MOSTLY GHOSTS

The

Three Spirits

of

Vandermeer Manor

YEARLING BOOKS/YOUNG YEARLINGS/YEARLING CLASSICS are designed especially to entertain and enlighten young people. Patricia Reilly Giff, consultant to this series, received the bachelor's degree from Marymount College. She holds the master's degree in history from St. John's University, and a Professional Diploma in Reading from Hofstra University. She was a teacher and reading consultant for many years, and is the author of numerous books for young readers.

For a complete listing of all Yearling titles, write to
Dell Readers Service, P.O. Box 1045,
South Holland, IL 60473.

MOSTLY GHOSTS

The
Three Spirits
of
Vandermeer Manor

by Mary Anderson

A YEARLING BOOK

Published by
Dell Publishing
a division of
Bantam Doubleday Dell Publishing Group, Inc.
666 Fifth Avenue
New York, New York 10103

Yearling ® TM 913705, Dell Publishing Co., Inc.

The trademark Yearling® is registered in the U.S. Patent
and Trademark Office.

ISBN: 0-440-48810-9

Printed in the United States of America

December 1987

10 9 8 7 6 5 4 3

CW

Chapter One

"HAVE YOU EVER SEEN A REAL BLACK SHEEP?" AMY SAID, watching the lush green trees that came into view as the Trailways bus sped along the highway.

"Guess not," Jamie answered. "Why'd you ask?"

"Dad always refers to Uncle Harold as a black sheep, so I wondered if they exist."

"Uncle Harry can't be that bad," Jamie said, "or Dad wouldn't let us spend our vacation with him."

Amy wasn't certain.

The twins had not seen their uncle in four years, not since their eighth birthday when Harold had given them each a wooden saber he had brought back from Thailand. Uncle Harold was always traveling around the world on business, and Amy could still recall what he had said when they opened their packages. "Those sabers come

1

from a country that used to be called Siam," he had explained with a twinkle in his eye. "That's why I thought they'd be appropriate. Siam—Siamese *twins*—get it?" Then he had guffawed. The twins' parents had considered the gifts in "questionable taste" and had stored them in the attic. Uncle Harold was always playing weird jokes or doing something out of the ordinary!

The mountains now appeared in the distance, and Amy was struck by the beauty of the Catskill area. But somehow she had misgivings about their journey.

"Do you think we're going to enjoy staying with Uncle Harold?"

Jamie didn't like the sound in his sister's voice. "You're not getting one of your psychic twinges, are you?" he asked, suddenly uneasy. "I mean, you don't think something weird is going to happen while we're at the Manor, do you?" Jamie was often resentful of his sister's psychic ability yet knew her premonitions were always right. "Well—do you?"

Something about Vandermeer Manor bothered Amy, though she wasn't certain what it was. Uncle Harold had sent them lots of pictures of the place after he had restored the old house. He had invested more than a year in returning it to its former grandeur, not to mention the "more than a million bucks" he had pumped into the restoration.

When Amy had first seen the pictures, she sensed something terribly sad and scary about the old house—as if someone had been extremely unhappy there. "I'm sure the Manor will be an interesting place to spend our vacation," she replied evasively, "but I never thought of Uncle Harold as a businessman. Dad says he's a child. Arrested development, Dad says."

"No way," Jamie argued. "Harold has made piles of money."

"Sheer luck, Dad says."

Jamie shrugged. "Sibling rivalry, *I* say. After all, Harold is younger than Dad and much more successful. Dad is just a history professor, but Uncle Harry is—well, I guess he's a tycoon. He owns property all over the world. We could all take lessons from Harry."

Jamie had been struggling with career possibilities, trying to determine what would best suit his superior academic talents. He had recently narrowed it down to whatever would make him tons of money. Secretly he had decided that Uncle Harold would be his role model. Whatever little tips Jamie might pick up during their vacation could help mold his future financial success.

Jamie leaned back in his seat and propped his knapsack behind his head. "Do you think the Manor has room service?"

"I suppose so."

"Great, we can call down at midnight and have ice-cream sodas delivered on a silver tray. Or maybe we can get hamburgers at two in the morning. This sure beats Camp Sycamore. We'll have marble bathrooms instead of mildewed cots."

"Remember what Mom said; we're not to take advantage."

"Why not?" Jamie asked. "We're Uncle Harry's guests. We can live like kings; he said so."

Amy stared out the window in silence as the afternoon sunlight fell across the mountains. She wouldn't dare admit it, but she felt a little homesick. She also missed the ghost of their ancestor Jebediah Aloysious Tredwell. The lieutenant colonel had not materialized in a while, but Amy knew that his spirit was somewhere near their house, and so she felt protected. In many ways Jeb wasn't a ghost at all; no, he was a dear friend who just happened to be a two-hundred-year-old spirit.

Jamie noticed the wistful expression on his sister's face. "What's wrong? You look like you swallowed a frog." He propped his feet up on the empty seat in front of them. "Be like me, relax and enjoy the ride. In another hour we'll be living in the lap of luxury, with not a care in the world—it'll be a true vacation."

"Sounds great," Amy said, then lapsed into thoughtful silence. Something deep inside her told her their bus was drawing them toward a tragic sorrow from the past.

Amy pushed the thought from her mind as she watched the passing scenery. The driver carefully maneuvered the bus up a road cut along a cliff that jutted down the hillside, exposing the beauty of the Hudson River valley. As they passed through towns with the colorful names Saugerties, Wappingers Falls, and Oneonta, the mountains grew closer and more imposing.

"Our stop is next," said Jamie excitedly. "I can hardly wait!"

4

Chapter Two

UNCLE HAROLD, DRESSED IN FADED KHAKI SHORTS, A RIPPED T-shirt, and a weathered fishing cap, was waiting for the twins at the bus station.

Amy quickly realized why her dad always referred to his younger brother as a child. Harold was in his early forties but seemed to be hiding behind the face of a boy—a rather naughty, mischievous boy.

Harold, his face sunburned and his nose peeling, waved enthusiastically as the twins got off the bus. "Over here, guys," he shouted, pointing to a bright red sports car. "Dump your gear in the back there and hop in."

Jamie whistled in admiration. "You're kidding—a *Porsche*? What does it do on the road?"

Uncle Harold laughed proudly. "Anything I tell it."

Amy was reluctant to mess up the fancy suede upholstery with their grubby suitcase and knapsacks, so she propped them on her lap.

"Don't worry," said Harold, "I've got much jazzier cars; this is my knockabout. Listen, if there's anything you forgot, replace it with new stuff in town. Charge whatever you need to my account."

Those words were music to Jamie's ears. "Well, we did forget our tennis rackets."

"No problem," said Harold. "While you're here, everything is on me. I want you kids to live like kings!"

"I knew this vacation would be great," Jamie said, sliding into the front seat next to his uncle.

Harold turned on the ignition, and the car took off like a bullet with the passing scenery flashing by.

"I can't wait to see the Manor," Jamie said.

"You've never seen anything like it," Harold said. "No one has in two hundred years. I've restored every last brick and beam. It's just the way it was when the last patroon, Jan Vandermeer, built the estate."

"What's a patroon?" Amy asked.

"Well," her uncle explained, "patroons were actually feudal lords. In the seventeenth century the first patroon, Kiliaen Vandermeer, owned the entire county—a hundred and fifty thousand acres clear up to Albany. His property was established under old Dutch grants, and the Vandermeers held this land for generations. Most of the property adjoining the Manor is now a state park and preserve. This area gets over fifty thousand visitors each year, and I'm betting lots of them will want to stay at the

Manor. Wait until you see the place, kids, it'll knock your eyes out."

"Did you really put in marble bathtubs?" Jamie asked.

"Sure, I added lots of modern conveniences, but essentially everything is just the way it was when Saskia Vandermeer lived there in the eighteenth century. According to local legends, she was quite a woman and a notorious spendthrift."

Amy felt a disturbing psychic twinge when she heard the name Saskia Vandermeer: it represented something *evil*. "She wasn't a nice person, was she, Uncle Harold?"

Amy's uncle stared at her in the rearview mirror. "Where'd you hear that? Have you been listening to the local legends already?"

"What legends?" Jamie asked. "*I* haven't heard anything."

Uncle Harold smiled impishly. "You're in Rip van Winkle country now, kids. There are tons of legends about ghosts and spirits up here. It's part of the Catskill Mountains' local color."

"Then Amy will feel right at home," Jamie said sarcastically. "She has a personal interest in *ghosts*."

Amy glared at her brother. Would he reveal the secret he'd sworn to keep forever? Would he blab that her psychic ability enabled her to conjure up their ancestor Jebediah? No, she realized; he was only teasing.

"So you like ghosts," Harold said with interest. "That's good because I'm hoping to make the ghost of Saskia Vandermeer big business in these parts."

Jamie was curious. "How can a ghost be big business?"

7

"Just wait," Harold said slyly, "you'll see."

As Harold raced his sports car along the highway, Jamie looked on admiringly. His instinct had been correct: there was lots to learn from Uncle Harry about money-making.

"We're almost there," said Harold. "Once we pass Rattlesnake Cliff and Chanooga Falls, we come to my property. The season hasn't started yet, so there are only fifteen guests at the Manor. Looks like you kids can have the rooms of your choice."

"With room service?" Jamie asked hopefully.

"You bet. This'll be a vacation to remember, I promise."

In the distance Amy could see the gables of a majestic manor house peeping through the trees on the nearby mountaintop.

"There she is," Harold said proudly. "Vandermeer Manor, the jewel of the Hudson River valley." As they neared the entrance to the estate, Harold slowed down the car and stopped by the iron gates.

The gatekeeper smiled and greeted him. "Afternoon, sir."

"Afternoon, Jake. Meet my niece and nephew, Amy and Jamie Ferguson. Treat them like royalty while they're here, okay?"

Jake tipped his hat. "Whatever you say, sir." He opened the huge metal gates, and Harold drove down a winding road lined with willow trees until they reached the manor house.

It was without a doubt the most spectacular house Amy had ever seen. It had massive wooden balconies and verandas surrounding all four sides. The property overlooked a narrow lake. Mountains and cliffs rose in the distance.

"What do you think?" Harold asked eagerly. "Fifty-four rooms with a panoramic view from every window."

"Fantastic," Jamie said. "A palace."

"Right," his uncle said. "Jan Vandermeer knew how to live. I got hold of his original blueprints for the place and copied everything exactly."

As the twins hurried from the car, a round, rosy-cheeked woman with gray hair stood on the lawn and waved to them.

"That's Bridget O'Flynn, our cook," Harold explained. "She'll take care of you guys if you need any mothering. Bridget raised eight of her own in the old country. I kidnapped her from an Irish castle, you know."

Bridget O'Flynn came hurrying down the path to greet them. "Such fine big children." She beamed and patted the twins on the back. "Master Harold told me all about the both of you."

"And I've told them all about you, Bridget. The jewel of the Emerald Isle is now the pride of the Hudson Valley."

"Away with you," she said, blushing. "The children only just arrived and already you're throwing the blarney," she added in her rich Irish brogue.

"But it's all true, Bridget me love," said Harold, mimicking her accent. "She was a cook in an Irish castle that had been turned into a hotel," he explained to the twins. "I snatched her away and promised to build her the finest kitchen in the county if she'd come to work for me."

"And you kept your word, Master Harold," Bridget said, and winked. "It's proud I am to cook in such a fine kitchen."

"Then rustle up these kids some of your famous Irish soda bread, okay?"

"No sooner said than done, sir. There's a fresh batch in the oven that only needs slicing." Bridget gave the twins a firm handshake before hurrying away.

"That woman *is* a jewel," Harold said, glancing after her. "She cares for her kitchen as if it were a baby. But heaven help anyone who tries to set foot into the sanctuary, so take warning, kids."

"Does Bridget make all the meals at the Manor?" Amy asked.

"Sure. So far we don't have too many guests, but Bridget is prepared for an army. As a girl in Killarney, she cooked for twelve brothers and sisters. I think she was born with a wooden spoon in her hand!" Harold wrapped his arms around the twins' shoulders. "Now let me show off *my* baby, okay?"

Harold eagerly ushered Amy and Jamie into the oak-paneled lobby of the manor house. Plush red carpeting covered the floors, and antique portraits hung on the brocaded walls. Each of the main rooms downstairs had huge bay windows that looked out over the lake. In the East Room, used as a recreational area, there was a marble fireplace and crystal chandeliers. Down the hall was an outer courtyard filled with rare exotic plants. Beyond this was the huge Dining Hall with heavy mahogany paneling, beamed ceilings, and an even larger fireplace inlaid with tiles.

Uncle Harold was an enthusiastic tour guide, showing off every feature of the building. "The original manor house was built in 1660 by Kiliaen Vandermeer," he explained. "Jan Vandermeer, his descendant, rebuilt the place in 1763." Harold pointed out the delicate ornamental carvings on the stained-glass windows, the neweled staircase, and the base-crucks, cross-wings, and wind-braces. "I think the Vandermeers modeled the building after medieval timber houses," he explained. "See the cornices around this truss-raftered roof? All hand-carved and every piece of wood flown over from Britain."

Sun poured through the bay windows, illuminating all the carved figures along the corners of the walls. The twins were definitely impressed. The terms Uncle Harold used to describe his reconstruction made no sense to them, but the results were obvious. The house was splendid. "It's the most beautiful house I've ever seen," said Amy.

"Listen," Jamie said. "The ceilings are so high, our voices echo. This Vandermeer guy must've had an awfully big family to fill up this place."

"No," said Harold, "just himself and his wife. Naturally, they had tons of servants."

"What'd you say he was again?"

"He was a patroon, Jamie."

"Oh, yeah. Well, patroons sure knew how to live!"

Uncle Harold was like a child showing off his latest

toy; he was clearly delighted the twins were so impressed with it. "Before I give you a grand tour of the upstairs, how about some of that Irish soda bread. Bridget has a table set in the Luncheon Hall."

The Luncheon Hall was only half the size of the great Dining Hall, and far less formal. Several guests were seated at tables covered with linen cloths. An arrangement of fresh wildflowers had been placed on each table. Two elderly ladies smiled and nodded as Harold entered.

"Good afternoon, Mr. Ferguson," one lady said.

"Afternoon, ladies," Harold said. "Excuse my appearance, I promise to be suitably dressed when I join you for dinner."

The older of the two women seemed delighted. "Oh? Will you be joining us for dinner?"

"Naturally, Miss Pettibone. A hotel owner is like the captain of a ship, you know. He should always join his charming guests for dinner."

Jamie nudged his sister. "Uncle Harry knows how to pour on the charm."

"I trust you ladies are enjoying your lunch?" Harold said.

The women nodded. "The trout was superb," they chorused.

"Fresh from the brook this morning and lovingly prepared by Bridget," Harold explained.

"You're right," Amy whispered to her brother. "Harold is a sweet-talker." She suspected he might be a bit of a con artist too!

A waitress placed the soda bread on the table. The

round loaf was still warm from the oven. Harold poured the twins tall icy glasses of lemonade.

"Staying here is going to be lots of fun," Jamie said, and gulped down his lemonade.

"Just wait until tonight," Harold said, "that's when the fun really begins."

Amy noticed a mischievous twinkle in her uncle's eye. "What do you mean?"

"Enough said for now," he replied, grinning. "You'll soon find out."

When they had finished eating, Harold insisted they see the portrait in the Dining Hall. "I forgot to show it to you, and it's a part of the grand tour."

On a corner wall, hanging in an ornate gilt frame, was the life-size painting of a woman. She was a beautiful woman, but the cold imperious look in her icy blue eyes made Amy shudder. "So that's Saskia Vandermeer."

"How'd you know that?" her uncle asked.

"Just a guess," Amy replied, but it was more than that. The moment Amy saw the portrait she knew there was something ominous about the former lady of the Manor.

"Yes, it's Saskia," Harold said, "the last mistress of the Manor. She vowed no one would follow after her, and she was right."

Madame Vandermeer peered out from her portrait, as if to say indeed she was *still* mistress of the Manor. Soft brown curls spilled around her shoulders. She wore a pale blue satin gown with a low bodice and fluttering ruffles at the elbow and sleeves. Its long skirt was elaborately festooned with lace and artificial flowers. In her hair she wore a headdress of ostrich plumes and ribbons.

"Some say her spirit still haunts this house," Harold continued. "Many of the locals swear they still hear her sing at night and play her harpsichord."

"That harpsichord?" Jamie asked, pointing to the instrument by the bay windows.

"Yes, that was Saskia's pride and joy. She had it shipped over from Holland as part of her dowry. I had all the strings replaced by craftsmen in Antwerp. Legend has it she played it every night, just after dinner. Some say the sound of her voice was so beautiful, it still rings across the mountains."

"Hey, what are you telling us, Uncle Harry?" asked Jamie. "Do you believe that legend? Do you think Saskia is still hanging around here?"

Harold seemed to find the question amusing. "Could be. What do *you* think?"

"I think I'd like to see my room," Jamie said, anxious to change the subject. Jamie already knew one ghost, and that was quite enough! Unlike his sister, he had never *seen* Jebediah Tredwell, but he had *heard* him. And it was Jamie's considered opinion that ghosts brought bad news, which he could do without on vacation. He would rather see the marble bathtub.

"Sure," Harold said, "you kids must be tired after your long trip. I'll give you adjoining rooms on the third floor of the East Wing. There's a spectacular view of Mohawk Mountain from there."

As they went upstairs Uncle Harold pointed out the

new architectural additions to the Manor, including the paneled elevator.

Both the children's rooms had a four-poster bed and a veranda overlooking the mountains, not to mention a pink and black marble bathroom. "Every piece was imported from Tuscany," Harold explained.

"Now I really do feel like a king!" Jamie said admiringly.

Harold seemed pleased. "Enjoy your reign. Listen, I've a million things to do, but I'll see you at dinner, okay? Seven o'clock in the Dining Hall. Dress is optional as long as it's not sneakers. I like to keep up a certain image."

"What'll we do first?" Jamie asked.

"Personally," Amy said, putting down her knapsack, "I'd like a long bubble bath in that marble tub."

"I think I'll write a letter to Elliot Bateman," Jamie said.

"To Elliot? What for?"

"Remember how he kept bragging about going to Malibu? Well, I'm writing to let him know what he's missing not being *here*. I'm also telling him Uncle Harry is the greatest guy in the world!"

Chapter Three

AFTER A RELAXING BATH, AMY SAT ON THE VERANDA AND watched the purple shades of dusk filter across the mountains. The hills in the west dipped suddenly into a narrow valley. Across the valley hills rose again in higher crests toward the mountains. Every few moments seemed to produce some magical change of color and shape. Then the setting sun slowly disappeared beyond the mountaintops, and mist began rolling across the hills.

As Amy admired the majestic scenery, she had an odd feeling: A certain danger hovered threateningly over Vandermeer Manor.

A chilly wind blew past her, and Amy shivered. As she turned to reenter her room the mist from the mountains seemed to follow her. Wisps of vapor swirled in front of her, then they began to crystallize, until the spirit of

Jebediah Aloysious Tredwell was standing before her. As usual, the lieutenant colonel wore the uniform of an officer in the Continental army, complete with tricornered hat, epaulets, sparkling brass buttons, and white gloves.

"Jeb!" Amy gasped in surprise. "What are you doing here?"

"Overseeing your welfare, Cousin," he replied. "As ever, as always."

"You are?" she asked. "I didn't realize you could leave Monroe. You once told me you always stayed close to your old apple orchard."

"And so I do, child," he answered. "And so I am," he added.

"How can that be, Jeb? If you're here, you can't be there, too—can you?"

"A spirit's movement can be as rapid as a thought," he explained. "Thus I may appear to be in several places at once."

"But how? Amy asked. "How can you split yourself up like that?"

"List, Cousin. The sun is only one body, yet it radiates in all directions, does it not? It sends out rays over great distances, yet it is not divided. So, too, with spirits."

"I don't understand that," Amy said truthfully.

"Do not fret," Jebediah said reassuringly. "Many things cannot be understood by man in this world, yet they are so."

"Well, I'm glad you're here, however you managed it.

Even though this is a beautiful place, something about it bothers me."

"And well it should," Jebediah said. "We stand upon land once owned by Kiliaen Vandermeer. His rule was an agrarian anachronism, and all those who fought or died for this country's freedom should find it odious. A desire for self-determination lies deep within the human heart, my child." Jebediah stood in stiff military fashion, one hand clasping the sword by his side. With his other hand he pointed out over the veranda. "There are spirits in these mountains and below within the valley who can testify to injustices during the reign of the Vandermeers. They know too well that no man can call himself free while he suffers the tyranny of another."

"What are you saying, Jeb? You mean there are ghosts around here?"

"Spirits exist everywhere," he explained. "Some wish to do you well and others do not. Therefore one must know their intent before one succumbs to their powers."

"You mean evil powers?" Amy asked.

"I fear I can say little more," Jebediah said. "Sadly, I may only reply according to the level of your understanding. But take note, Cousin. If evil spirits exist, it is in this imperfect world they are to be found, for spirits of a lower degree flourish here."

"Low-grade spirits?" Amy said. "That doesn't sound good. What do they want? I'll bet you mean Saskia Vandermeer! I've got this creepy feeling about her, Jeb. Uncle Harold says people swear she haunts this place."

"Beware spirits of the third order," Jebediah warned. "They can assume a pleasing mask in order to deceive."

"The third order? What's that?"

"I can say no more for now," Jebediah replied. "Time will reveal what I cannot."

Lieutenant Colonel Tredwell now began to disappear as quickly as he had materialzed.

"No, wait," Amy said pleadingly. "You've got to tell me *more*."

But it was too late. Jebediah's spirit had already transformed itself into a vapory mist which now wafted out over the veranda, mingling with the mist floating in from the mountains.

Amy grumbled to herself and sat down on the bed just as Jamie rushed through the door.

"Well, what do you think?" he asked, posing casually in the doorway. He was wearing his new tan slacks, suede loafers, and a white cotton sweater. "Is this fancy enough for Vandermeer Manor?"

Amy did not answer. Glancing toward the veranda, she stared out over the mountains.

"What's with you?" Jamie asked. "Why are you still in your bathrobe? Hurry and dress for dinner."

"Jebediah was just here," Amy said solemnly.

"Jeb? Here? Just now?"

Amy nodded.

And Jamie groaned as his enthusiasm for the upcoming evening quickly began to fade. Jeb, he knew, always appeared to warn them about something. "What's it this time? Werewolves? Leprechauns? Man-eating plants? What danger are we supposed to be in now?"

"Quit joking, you know Jebediah is always right. He's our spirit guide and only wants to help us."

"Okay, so what did he tell you?"

"I couldn't understand him," she said truthfully, "I *never* do. But it's got something to do with Saskia Vandermeer. I think Jeb said she was a third-rate, low-class spirit."

"A what?"

"Something like that, honestly. If you'd been here, you could've heard him yourself."

"Some good that'd do me," Jamie complained. "I've never seen the guy and can barely hear him. Jeb comes in like a radio signal bounced off Mars—all garbled up."

"I got his message garbled, too, Amy confessed, "but I think he came to warn us. Something creepy must be going on here."

"Forget it," Jamie said. "If there's some third-rate spirit hanging around this place, so what? It's not our business. C'mon, hurry up and get dressed for dinner."

"You're right," Amy said, "nothing is going to ruin this vacation!"

Chapter Four

THE SMALL ASSEMBLY OF GUESTS AT VANDERMEER MANOR were already seated in the huge Dining Hall.

A waitress escorted the twins toward a table near the balcony. "Your uncle will join you soon," she explained, removing the Reserved sign. "My name's Judy. Would you kids like drinks? When I was your age, I loved Shirley Temples."

Jamie almost blushed. He felt like ordering a scotch on the rocks just to see the waitress's expression. "Some cola, please," he said huskily. Amy ordered the same.

As the sounds of clattering dinner plates echoed through the massive space of the great Dining Hall, Jamie admired his surroundings. The huge crystal chandelier shimmered and the well-oiled mahogany paneling gleamed. A silver candelabrum had been placed upon the harpsi-

21

chord. The large French doors behind it were closed to keep out the cool mountain breezes.

"Uncle Harold did a great job on this place," said Jamie. "Sitting here makes me feel I'm back in the Eighteenth century."

Amy stared at the portrait of Saskia Vandermeer. The lights from the chandelier softened the pale blue color of her satin gown but did nothing to soften the stern expression on the face of the former mistress of the Manor. Saskia looked out over the assembled crowd in the Dining Hall like a queen disdainfully regarding her subjects. Amy stared at her thoughtfully. "How could a woman who looked so regal be low-class?" she wondered out loud.

"Forget that junk Jeb told you," said Jamie, glancing at the menu. "We're here to enjoy ourselves, remember? Should I order pork chops or chicken Kiev?"

Harold approached the table. "Why not order filet mignon," he suggested. It's our most expensive entree."

"Then I'll have it," said Jamie.

Harold laughed admiringly. "You're a young man who knows the value of things. You remind me of myself when I was young." Uncle Harold looked surprisingly formal in his white linen jacket and black satin tie. He pulled up a chair and sat between the twins. "Is everything satisfactory so far?"

"Everything's great," said Jamie. "I took a walk earlier and saw the clay tennis courts; they're terrific. I'll bet you imported the clay from someplace, right?"

Harold laughed again. "No, it's strictly local clay. I'll be glad to play a few sets with you once we get you that new raquet."

"You're dressed very nicely, Uncle Harold," Amy observed.

"Special attire for a special occasion," he explained. "After all, I have special visitors. You two have come from Monroe and—well, who knows what other illustrious persons might show up," he added mysteriously.

Amy realized her uncle had been hinting at something all day. "Are you expecting someone else?" she asked.

Uncle Harold unfolded his napkin, then glanced at the menu. "One never knows," he replied, refusing to elaborate.

The twins had finished their main courses and had just begun their apple cobblers when Uncle Harold suddenly stood up and clinked the side of his glass. "Guests of the Manor," he announced, "may I have your attention, please."

All the guests looked up from their meals, turned in their chairs, and glanced at Harold.

"I hope you're all enjoying your stay here," he went on. "Since this is our opening week, I'd like you each to have a glass of champagne, compliments of the house."

In unison, the guests applauded with gratitude as waitresses approached their tables carrying trays of champagne-filled glasses.

"I've timed the opening of Vandermeer Manor to correspond with a historic date," Harold continued. "On this very day, two hundred twenty-five years ago, Saskia Vandermeer became mistress of this Manor. I'm sure you've all admired her portrait and heard the legends of her occasional return visits to her dear old homestead."

"We certainly have," said a bald man at a corner table. "Me and the missus were hoping the old girl might show up while we were here."

A woman at another table giggled in agreement. "I was hoping that myself."

"My husband and I were thinking the same thing," confessed a woman seated nearby.

All the guests seemed to agree that seeing a real ghost during their vacation would make their trip especially memorable.

"Well, you never know," said Harold. "I've heard all the legends too. Folks around here say that every night at nine Saskia would sit down to play that harpsichord over there. Naturally I can't promise anything, but I have this strange premonition that she's around here somewhere tonight."

"You do, Mr. Ferguson?" one elderly woman asked. "Really? How exciting."

"Yes, indeed, ma'am," said Harold, rubbing his hands together. "It's a definite premonition."

Jamie nudged his sister. "I guess Uncle Harry is psychic too," he whispered. "Maybe it runs in the family."

"I'm sure no one here is afraid of ghosts," the bald man said, "but maybe the little lady is afraid of *us*. You think she'd show herself to such a crowd?"

"She might," Harold said, "if we made her feel at

home. Maybe if we dimmed the lights and sat quietly, she'd appear. Would anyone object to finishing their meal by candlelight?"

The guests agreed Harold's suggestion was both appropriate and romantic, so the lights were quickly turned off. Waitresses lit the candles at each table as Harold lit the candelabra on the harpsichord. Then the guests resumed their meal, eagerly hoping that Saskia Vandermeer might see fit to grace them with her presence. With the dimming of the lights the dinner conversation became more hushed.

On exactly the stroke of nine the grandfather clock in the Main Hall began to chime. With each succeeding chime the possibility of the ghost's appearance became more imminent.

Muffled whispers began to pass from one table to another as all the guests anticipated the arrival of their historic visitor. "I hope she comes." "I'm sure she'll come." "I can't wait to see her."

The tension within the room mounted.

With the ninth chime of the clock the French doors suddenly swung open. The guests gasped with excitement and glanced toward the balcony.

At first all anyone could see was a thin crescent moon beyond the blackness of the mountains. But then they heard the faintest humming; a far-off sound, it was a woman's voice.

Then they saw her standing there in the doorway: Saskia Vandermeer. A strange unearthly glow surrounded her. A figure seemingly composed entirely of particles of light, she looked real yet at the same time oddly unreal. Soft candlelight fell upon her icy-blue satin gown. The cool evening breeze gently rustled the ostrich plumes in her beribboned headdress.

As Saskia glanced around the room, she became aware of the guests assembled within. Her eyes set upon the harpsichord in the corner, and she smiled. She seemed to float toward it, her feet barely touching the ground, and then she sat upon the velvet stool and began to play.

And as she played, Saskia sang. Her voice had a beautiful bell-like clarity. Her pale white fingers caressed the keys, and her opal ring glowed in the candlelight. The harpsichord emitted a soulful baroque melody—a haunting, ageless tune that might have been filtering across the mountains for centuries.

The guests in the Dining Hall sat motionless as they listened. No one moved, no one spoke. Everyone seemed afraid that one movement might break the spell and the lovely vision would vanish. Saskia played on, just as she had done every evening when she was mistress of the Manor. In the mahogany-paneled Dining Hall lit by the candelabra, the clock had been turned back to a quieter, simpler time when Saskia Vandermeer reigned supreme.

And then the music ceased. Saskia closed the lid of the harpsichord, pushed out the velvet stool, then stood up and slowly exited through the French doors. She was gone. A breeze blew through the window, extinguishing the flames of the candelabra.

Harold sighed. "I think we can turn the lights back on

now," he said, hurrying toward the wall switch. "That seems to be it for this evening."

As the chandelier was switched back on, the guests felt themselves projected forward into the present, and the magical mood was broken.

"That was terrific," the bald man said.

"Yes," a woman said, "a truly profound experience."

"A privilege," added another.

"Something to tell our grandchildren about."

"Do you think she'll come again?"

All the guests were so excited, they now began to talk in unison. They were anxious to share the experience, to compare their feelings, and thrilled they had all witnessed it together. In addition, everyone felt they owed a personal debt of gratitude to Harold Ferguson.

"Saskia appeared because you restored this place so beautifully," one guest suggested.

"Yes," another said, "you made her feel at home here again."

Harold smiled humbly. "Maybe that means she'll appear again."

"I'm sure of it," the bald man said, "but I wouldn't have believed it if I hadn't seen it for myself."

"Let's tell all our friends about this place," someone suggested.

Each of the guests shook Harold's hand as he mingled among them, graciously accepting their compliments.

Jamie was excited too. "That's what I call a *real* ghost, not like Jeb. I could see and hear everything clear as a bell. Do you think people are right? Could Uncle Harry be responsible?"

"I'm afraid so," Amy said.

"What's that mean?"

Amy was reluctant to elaborate. "I hate to say this, Jamie, but I don't think we saw a real ghost."

Chapter Five

THE SATISFIED GUESTS HAD ALL RETIRED FOR THE NIGHT, AND so had Uncle Harold.

Jamie, unable to resist room service, ordered some cookies and a pot of cocoa as a midnight snack. When it arrived he insisted Amy come to his room to talk. "First you tell me Jeb warned you about a ghost up here, then we actually see a ghost up here and then you say it wasn't a ghost at all. Are you nuts, or what?"

"No, but I'm *psychic*, which means I know a ghost when I see one."

"Excuse me! So you're the only one in the world who can see ghosts, right?"

"Look, when a ghost appears, a funny thing happens inside me. It's like an electric current, and it didn't happen tonight."

Jamie gobbled a cookie, then said, "Maybe you've got a short circuit. Everyone else saw the ghost and they all believed it, didn't they?"

"Yes, but maybe they *wanted* to."

Jamie wanted to be reasonable. "Okay, if it wasn't a ghost, it was a real person, right? And if it was a real person, she was pretending—which means it was a *performance*."

Amy nodded. "A performance staged by Uncle Harold, I'm afraid. He hinted about it all day, remember?"

"But why should Uncle Harry stage something like that?"

"Can't you guess?"

"Sure I can," Jamie said. "It'd mean big business for the Manor, right?"

"Right. Once the word gets around there's a friendly ghost up here, the place will be packed—which it isn't now."

"Okay," Jamie said, "maybe you're right. *Maybe* Uncle Harry staged this for publicity, but I'd need proof before I come to that conclusion."

"I hope I'm wrong," Amy said, stifling a yawn, "but I have no proof either way, so I'm going to bed."

As his sister left the room Jamie stared out the window. If Uncle Harry *had* staged the whole deal, he was an even better businessman than Jamie had imagined. There certainly was lots to learn from good old Uncle Harry!

The next morning at breakfast Bridget O'Flynn came to the twins' table. "Your uncle is off goodness knows where," she explained, "so I'm making sure you select a good meal. I hope you're hungry."

"Always," Jamie said, "and I always eat a big breakfast."

Bridget pinched his cheek. "You're a boy after my own heart. I'll see you get an extrabig portion." She slid into the chair beside Jamie. "I'm just after hearing what happened last night. The whole staff is buzzing about it."

"You mean the ghost?" he asked.

" 'Tis lucky we are it's a friendly ghost," Bridget said, and nodded. "Irish castles are filled with the likes of them. Pay them no mind and they go about their business."

"Really?" Jamie said.

"You've seen ghosts too?" Amy asked.

"What self-respecting Irishwoman hasn't? Sure and I'm not too old to remember the first one ever I saw. Clancy O'Reilly it was. We'd no sooner given Clancy his wake than he was up and dancing with the rest of us. Dead he was an hour before, as dead as a mackerel in a fish market. But Clancy could never pass up a good jig," Bridget added.

"You're not *afraid* of ghosts?" Jamie asked.

"Ghosts are just like people," Bridget said philosophically. "Most are good but a few are bad, so I'd count my blessings."

As Bridget left, Jamie poked his sister. "See? Bridget is an expert, too, and she believes it."

"Okay," Amy said, "I guess I'm wrong." It made her uncomfortable to regard her uncle Harold with suspicion, and so she wanted to drop the whole subject. But as

31

she stared across the room she was convinced her suspicions were accurate. A young woman dressed in a jogging outfit had just sat down at the opposite table. She glanced around furtively, then quickly buried her face inside a magazine. "Jamie, if you still want proof, look over there."

Jamie glanced at the woman. "She must be a new guest, I didn't see her here last night."

"Yes you did, look closer."

Jamie looked again. The woman had a suntan and wore her hair in a long ponytail. "No," he said, "I don't recognize her."

"I'll admit she's hard to recognize," Amy said, "but that ring she's wearing isn't." Amy stared at the large opal within its unusual filigree setting. "I admired that ring last night while Saskia was playing the harpsichord. I'd never forget a ring like that."

Jamie looked again. "You mean *she's*— No, it can't be. She doesn't look anything like the ghost."

"Imagine her in the proper lighting, with makeup and costume."

"Well, maybe so, I'm not sure."

"I am," Amy said, getting up, "and I'm going to speak to her." She went over to the woman's table, and Jamie followed. "We enjoyed your performance last night," she said politely.

The woman was caught off guard. "Thank you— I mean, whatever do you mean?"

"You sing very well," Amy continued, "and you play the harpsichord beautifully."

The woman blushed beneath her suntan. "I've no idea what you mean," she said haltingly. "I've just arrived this morning. You've mistaken me for someone else. What makes you think I performed here?"

"Your ring," Amy explained. "It's not in Saskia's portrait but she was wearing it last night."

"Oh, no," she said, quickly covering the ring with her hand, "Mr. Ferguson will kill me!"

Jamie quickly pulled up a chair and sat down. "So it *was* a setup! C'mon, tell us everything. This was all Uncle Harry's idea, right?"

"Are you related?" the woman asked. "Well, in that case— Look, I'm sorry I messed things up. Your uncle had the whole performance worked out so beautifully."

"Maybe you should tell us your real name," Amy said.

"I'm Cynthia Mallory. I'm an actress and I'm performing in a summer stock production up here. Your uncle saw our show and said he had a job for me if I could play the harpsichord. He hired me to appear in the Dining Hall every evening at nine to play and sing but never to speak to anyone."

"C'mon," Jamie said, "he must've told you you were supposed to be a ghost."

"Sure, but that was part of the challenge. I've never played a ghost before. It's a stretch, you know." Miss Mallory was clearly embarrassed by the children's questions. "Look, kids, it was just a job. Your uncle told me people would love going along with the fantasy, and he was right. He's paying me lots more than I get for a week's work in stock. Acting jobs are hard to find, you know."

"So are real ghosts," Jamie said.

"I haven't done anything wrong," Miss Mallory said defensively. She got up from the table just as the waitress arrived with the coffee. "It's just an acting job," she said nervously, "and perfectly respectable."

Then Cynthia Mallory brushed past the waitress and hurriedly left the room.

Another waitress entered carrying two huge platters of pancakes, sausages, and scrambled eggs. "Your breakfast," she told the twins.

"I think I've lost my appetite," Amy said.

"I haven't," Jamie said, digging into the sausages and hotcakes like someone who hadn't eaten in days.

The twins had waited all morning for their uncle's return, arguing over what to say to him. They had finally decided to confront him with all the facts.

To their surprise, Harold seemed remarkably unconcerned about their discovery. "So you've discovered my little deception, eh?" he said, propping his feet on the balcony railing and glancing out over the lake. "Well, I'm sure I can count on your discretion."

"Discretion?" Amy repeated. "You mean to keep things quiet?"

"Naturally. My guests are thrilled about the ghost. Word of mouth travels fast up here, and we've already got several bookings for next week. Before the month is out, this place will be jammed. You don't want to spoil everyone's fun, do you?"

Amy didn't want to spoil anything, but something told her that fooling around with phony spirits could unleash some dangerous force. "Don't you think you're cheating people?" she asked.

"Of course not. I'm giving them entertainment with their dinner, free of charge."

"That's true," Jamie said, "it's just like dinner theater."

"Exactly. People will remember their vacation here for the rest of their lives."

To Jamie, it all seemed like sound business reasoning. "Tell me, how'd you get Miss Mallory to look so much like a ghost?"

"I had the costume in the portrait copied," Harold explained proudly. "Cynthia wore a special translucent makeup. As for the rest, a little stage lighting installed on the balcony worked wonders."

"But she *floated* into the room," Jamie said.

Harold laughed. "Roller skates. No one saw them under Cynthia's costume, and they couldn't be heard on the carpeting. Special rubber wheels," he added, "which I got from a company that rents theatrical props."

"Brilliant," Jamie said admiringly. "A ghost on wheels, it's a riot. No wonder everyone was fooled."

"They actually fooled themselves," Harold said. "They *wanted* to believe in the ghost, so they did."

Their conversation was interrupted when Miss Pettibone strolled onto the veranda.

"Good day, Miss Pettibone," Harold said, smiling.

Miss Pettibone took a deep breath of mountain air and exhaled it slowly. "Inspired." She sighed. "My decision to come here was inspired, Mr. Ferguson. All my life I've wanted to see a ghost and now I have. I'm leaving tomorrow, so I do hope dear Saskia will appear again this evening."

"That's very possible," Harold said brightly. "I can assure you the spirit of Saskia Vandermeer is still around here—somewhere."

Chapter Six

UNCLE HAROLD WAS RIGHT: WORD TRAVELS QUICKLY IN THE mountains. The staff and guests had discussed the ghostly appearance all day, with amazing results. By that evening Vandermeer Manor had seven new guests. One of them, a Mr. Deutch, was a reporter for the *Hudson Valley Bulletin.* Rumors of a ghost-in-residence were of special interest to him, and he was eager to determine the spirit's "historic authenticity."

By seven-thirty the great Dining Hall was bustling with activity. "Business has picked up already," Harold said, beaming, "and everyone's ordering my most expensive wines. This place will be a success in no time!"

Jamie agreed. "Uncle Harry is right. Everyone is dying to see the ghost again."

Amy said nothing as she ate her dinner. She wanted to

take the whole thing lightly, as Jamie was doing, but she felt her uncle's innocent subterfuge could have disastrous results. Amy couldn't stop thinking about what Jeb had told her. Jeb's warnings were never given lightly—or without reason.

At eight-thirty guests began asking if the lights would be turned off again, and Uncle Harold obliged. All the candles were lit, and the guests finished their meal in semidarkness. Gradually the room settled into silence, and everyone waited expectantly.

Once again the chimes of the grandfather clock began to sound throughout the Manor. *Bong, bong, bong*, they rang out. A heavy silence enveloped the Dining Hall. *Bong, bong, bong*, they repeated. A sudden chill swept over the guests, and they shivered. *Bong, bong, bong* —and on the ninth chime the French doors swung open and the mist from the mountains rolled into the room. It was an eerie blue-white mist, which brought with it the odor of damp and mold.

Then once again Saskia Vandermeer appeared on the balcony. Her icy-blue satin gown shimmered in the candlelight. Her pale white skin seemed translucent. As she stepped through the doorway, the guests eagerly awaited the concert they assumed would soon commence.

But Saskia Vandermeer did not approach the harpsichord. Instead, she raised her hands above her head, and as she did so, a chilling gust of wind blew through the Dining Hall, extinguishing all the candles. Now the only light within the room emanated from the ghostly figure herself, standing defiantly in the center of the great hall.

Then slowly the lovely face of Saskia Vandermeer contorted into a hideous mask. She opened her mouth to speak, and angry words, like bolts of lightning, spilled from her lips in an unearthly demonic croak. "Do not defile that which is *mine*. Begone from my home!" Saskia raged. "Destruction to all those who do not obey!"

At first the guests stared, not comprehending, confused by the change in the spirit's mood, for it had been so hospitable the night before.

Then the rage within the spirit grew uncontrollable. Saskia raised her hands again, and a great gust of wind blew in through the French doors and overturned tables and chairs. The spirit emitted a guttural croaking laugh. "Begone," she repeated. "Only I reign here, and I shall unleash destruction on all intruders!"

One of the guests screamed in terror. That scream was followed by another and another, until everyone began to panic. As Harold rushed to switch on the lights, the spirit floated toward the French doors and disappeared into the evening mist.

Miss Pettibone was so distraught, she began to hyperventilate. The bald man came to her assistance while the other guests tried to regain control of themselves.

"I've never had such an awful experience," a young woman complained. "This place must be jinxed." All the guests agreed something evil had taken place. "I'm checking out as fast as I can," another person said.

Harold mingled with the guests, desperately trying to calm them down, but his efforts seemed in vain.

Jamie was stunned. "What happened to Miss Mallory? I never saw such overacting, she must've gone bonkers!"

Amy realized Jeb's warning had come to pass. "That wasn't Miss Mallory," she explained. "I'm afraid that was the real ghost of Saskia Vandermeer!"

After the guests had fled the Dining Hall, Uncle Harold began to realize the consequences of the evening's visit. "This is ridiculous," he grumbled, "my staff won't clean up here because they say the room is haunted. I told them they *knew* that already, but they say things are different now."

"We'll help you," Amy said, and began to stack the dinner plates.

"Sure," Jamie said, and started picking up the overturned chairs and tables.

"Thanks, kids," Harold said, putting the tables back in place. "That certainly was unexpected, wasn't it? I'll have to speak with Miss Mallory. She shouldn't have blown up her part like that. Tomorrow night she keeps her mouth shut and plays the harpsichord. I'm not paying her to ham it up. Half the guests were scared to death."

Amy stared at her uncle. "That wasn't Miss Mallory, we must've scared her off this afternoon. That was a *real* ghost!"

"Yeah, sure, and I'm the Easter bunny."

"She *was* real." Amy was insistent. "A true ectoplasmic manifestation. She must be very powerful for everyone to see her."

Jamie had to agree. "You'd better listen, Uncle Harry. Amy knows about stuff like that."

Harold grinned. "Stuff like what?"

"Ghosts and things," Jamie said.

Harold closed and latched the French doors. "Okay, kids, maybe I deserve to have my leg pulled. I'll admit my master plan backfired, but don't take a good joke too far."

"It was a true apparition," Amy said. "Saskia is probably the third-rate spirit I was warned about."

"Warned?" Harold repeated. "Who warned you?"

"I can't tell you that."

Harold chuckled. "Okay, kids, play your little game, I suppose I deserve it. Just remember you can't kid a kidder."

"I wish Amy was kidding, Uncle Harry, but she has a way of knowing these things."

Harold was growing impatient. "Okay, have it your own way. C'mon, I'm settling this thing once and for all."

The twins followed their uncle into the Main Hall, where he telephoned Miss Mallory at the Hudson Valley Lodge.

"Hi, Cynthia. Listen, about your performance tonight. You *what?* . . . You didn't show up? . . . What do you mean you *quit?* Stop fooling around, you were here an hour ago. . . . You *weren't?*" As Harold hung up the phone his hands were shaking. "I think I need a good stiff drink," he groaned.

*　　*　　*

41

After two glasses of brandy Harold was still shaky. "A *real* ghost and just my luck she doesn't like company. I'm ruined!"

"Don't take it so hard," Jamie said sympathetically. "So what if you lose a few guests, who cares? After all, you've lots of other business interests. This place could be a tax write-off for a big tycoon like you."

"This place is my *last chance*," Harold shouted. "I put every last dime I could beg or borrow into it. I owe *everyone*—including your father."

"You borrowed money from Dad?" Amy asked. "But why? You're a millionaire."

Harold sighed. "Past tense. I *was* a millionaire—but I've had some bad reversals the past two years. My oil wells came in dry, my stocks fell; now I'm in debt up to my eyeballs. Everything is riding on Vandermeer Manor. If that ghost returns, she'll scare away every guest I've got." Harold poured himself another drink. "I'm taking this one upstairs. Before I go to bed, I'm praying Saskia Vandermeer never comes back—which is ridiculous because I don't even *believe* in ghosts!"

Chapter Seven

"POOR UNCLE HAROLD," AMY SAID, "WE'VE GOT TO HELP him." She was sitting in her brother's room, unable to sleep. "How much money do you think Dad invested in this place?"

"A bundle, I bet. You know what a sweet-talker Uncle Harry is. Dad once told me Harry talked him out of every comic book he owned when they were kids. Harry *saved* them all, and years later he sold them to a collector."

Although Jamie still secretly admired his uncle's enterprise, he agreed he was in a big mess.

"Should I contact Jeb?" Amy asked.

"I suppose so. Maybe he'll know why Saskia Vandermeer is making such a fuss."

"Okay, I'll try," she said. Amy sat down on the floor and crossed her legs. "Sit beside me, Jamie," she said, closing her eyes. Concentrating all her energy, Amy began to visualize the spirit of Jebediah Aloysious Tredwell in her mind's eye. "Jeb, we need you," she whispered.

"Yeah, J.T.," added Jamie, "pop up if you're around."

"Jebediah Tredwell," Amy repeated the invocation, "we need your help."

A cool wave of energy passed across Amy's body and she opened her eyes. The lieutenant colonel was standing beside the four-poster bed, admiring its canopy. "Irish lace," he commented, rubbing a piece between his fingers. "It's made from the finest linen."

"Can you *feel* it?" Amy asked.

"Nope," said Jamie, "I don't feel a thing."

"Not *you*," Amy told him. "I'm not talking to you."

"Then who?" Jamie asked. He glanced in the direction of Amy's stare. As usual, he saw nothing. "You mean Jeb is here?"

"Yes." Amy nodded.

"Ask him why Saskia Vandermeer is haunting this place."

Jebediah Tredwell's spirit circled the bed, then sat on its edge. "It seems the lady of the Manor is still extremely territorial," he explained, "and most avaricious, just as she was in her lifetime. She has changed not a whit since the days when I knew her."

"You *knew* Saskia Vandermeer?" Amy asked.

Jebediah nodded. "I was a guest of Jan Vandermeer's on one occasion, during which time he gave me a tour of his baronial estate: an acreage forty-eight miles long and twenty-eight miles wide. His own flag with his family's

44

coat of arms flew above the Manor. Oh, yes, at one time this property included several thousand tenants and many slaves. Though all who are vassals are enslaved, do you not agree, Cousin? One cannot have a legally established government within another government, with prerogatives of sovereignty and baronial rights. It is the grossest contradiction."

Jamie could not hear a thing. "What's Jeb saying?"

Amy shrugged. "Don't ask me; he's talking funny again."

Jamie grew impatient. "There's no time for jokes, J.T. Can you help us or not? We've got a serious ghost problem."

" 'Tis serious indeed," the lieutenant colonel said. "But Saskia Vandermeer must not be your main concern. There is a far more troubled spirit in our midst—a truly tormented soul trapped between two planes, unable to cross over."

Jamie picked up some snatches of the conversation. "Who's trapped in an airplane?"

"Shhh," Amy said. "Jeb, do you mean there's another ghost living here too?"

"*Another* ghost?" Jamie asked.

" 'Tis regrettably so," Jebediah replied. "A spirit such as Madame Vandermeer is a frivolous sort who enjoys the little annoyances she may cause. Her advancement toward the knowledge of the infinite will take much time. But this other spirit to whom I refer cannot begin its journey, for it is still trapped in a netherworld. Mark me, Cousins, you must fear such a spirit as this. Unwittingly

45

it can cause great damage to corporal beings, for it possesses powers without proper knowledge. Take heed, children, everything in nature is linked together. To break that link can have cataclysmic results."

"Did Jeb say something about a stink?" Jamie said, obviously confused.

"Who is this other spirit?" Amy asked.

"It shall reveal itself presently. Therefore I warn you—be on guard."

Amy felt uneasy. "What does this spirit want?"

"Sadly, it knows not, for it still has a fluid peculiar to itself which it draws from the atmosphere of this planet. Unless you come to its aid, it is locked forever within its perispirit."

"Did Jeb say it was a *merry* spirit?" asked Jamie.

"Hardly," Amy said. "He says it's a troubled soul who can't pass on—and it's very *dangerous*."

"Terrific," Jamie groaned, "we've got a doubleheader."

"How can *we* help?" Amy asked.

"Paradoxically, you must protect yourselves from it yet give it assistance."

"How do we do that?"

"Cautiously," Jebediah said, "most cautiously. It is a soul in sorrowful torment. Be advised." With these words he slowly began to fade away. "Be advised."

Suddenly the lieutenant colonel disappeared before Amy's eyes. She shuddered with apprehension. "I'm *scared*, Jamie. There's a tormented ghost around here somewhere, and we're supposed to help it before it *hurts* us."

Jamie was angry. "That figures, right? We call on Jeb for help and he adds to our problems. Who's this ghost supposed to be anyhow?"

"Jeb didn't say."

"Swell. You think we should go looking for it?"

"Not me," Amy said, "no way. Don't trouble trouble until trouble troubles you. I'm going to bed."

"Me too," said Jamie, "but I'm keeping my lights on."

"Me too," Amy echoed.

Chapter Eight

THE CHILDREN HAD A RESTLESS NIGHT. AWAKE AT THE COMing of dawn, they hoped the tormented spirit Jeb had forewarned them about would postpone its appearance indefinitely.

The twins were still yawning when they took the elevator down to the Main Hall. There they noticed several suitcases lined up by the entrance, and that meant bad news for Uncle Harold.

"People are starting to check out," Amy said.

"I don't blame them," Jamie said. "Who needs a hotheaded ghost on a vacation? If they knew there was *another* one waiting in the wings . . ."

"Don't tell anyone, Jamie."

"Not me. This place is scary enough with people in it; I don't want it empty."

48

The five guests who had decided to remain temporarily were all seated at breakfast. None of them looked too cheerful.

"I guess they couldn't find other accommodations," observed Judy, the waitress. "Most of the staff gave notice this morning."

"How about you?" Amy asked.

"Me? Madame Vandermeer hasn't bothered me—not yet, anyway. Besides, there's gossip down in the kitchen. Some say there isn't any ghost at all. They think your uncle *staged* the whole thing."

"Really?" Jamie said. "How'd they find—I mean, how come?"

Judy was anxious to share her juicy bit of gossip. "Well," she said, leaning across the table, "one of the maids was cleaning up room two-twelve, see? It was empty, you know? Anyway, she noticed this gorgeous gown hanging in the closet . . . the same gown that's in that portrait in the Dining Hall. She found other stuff, too—stage makeup and things. She thinks Mr. Ferguson hired someone to *pretend* she was a ghost—an actress, maybe."

"No kidding," Amy said.

"You bet, so don't worry, kids. This place is as safe as it ever was. How about some nice hotcakes?"

As Judy was leaving, Uncle Harold joined them. He had dark circles under his eyes. "Too much brandy and no sleep," he explained.

"We didn't sleep, either," said Jamie, "not after we found out—"

Amy kicked her brother underneath the table. "Maybe

Saskia Vandermeer won't come back again," she said quickly. "I'll bet she was just angry because someone was playing her harpsichord."

"You think so?" Harold asked hopefully. "I hope you're right. We'll have to wait until tonight to find out."

Later that morning Harold drove the twins into town and bought them new tennis rackets—the most expensive ones available. Then he took them on a tour of the area.

Harold drove through the countryside, which was dotted with apple orchards and vineyards, then up a winding cliff road toward Heartbreak Falls. Their ears rang with the deafening roar of water falling over the precipice—in a steep descent into dark, stony depths. The twins clung to the pathway of lichen-covered rocks where moss and vines grew underfoot.

Amy found the falls spectacular but also a little frightening. "Where did it get its name?" she asked.

"From an Indian legend," Uncle Harold said. "Naturally, this was all Indian land until the Dutch bought it. A Mohican girl drowned here, I think. I'll bet Cliff Hightower knows the story."

"Who's he?" Jamie asked.

"Cliff owns a souvenir shop in town. He's part Indian and knows all the local legends. Folks say the Indian girl's ghost still haunts this place."

Amy stared at the misty veils of spray shooting out from the falls and remembered what Jebediah had told her: Many spirits haunt the Catskill Mountains and their valleys.

Uncle Harold drove them past Overlook Point, where they saw a panoramic view of the county. "Dutch settlers believed Henry Hudson kept vigil over the river from this spot," he explained. "If so, he had a great view."

Jamie agreed. "It's like being on top of the world."

On their ride back to the Manor they all sang camp songs. Uncle Harold was determined not to let "one cranky ghost" get the better of him. "I've been in tough financial spots before and I've always pulled out of them. How about some tennis later, kids?"

The twins were up for that. Jamie and Amy played the first set, then Uncle Harold took Jamie on.

"Are you sure you didn't *let* me win that last set?" Jamie was out of breath.

"I never let anyone win"—Harold was puffing as he spoke—"not if I can help it."

The day had been so warm and pleasantly eventful, the twins had abandoned all thoughts of ghosts and hauntings. But as it grew dark, gray storm clouds blew in over the mountains, and the mood turned somber. No one seemed anxious to enter the Dining Hall for dinner.

Harold, wearing his formal white linen jacket, once again performed his duties as host. He stopped by each table to greet the diners. With only five guests remaining, that did not take long.

"I feel so sorry for him," Jamie said, "this giant place is practically empty."

Harold returned to the table. "The guests seem to

51

think we were victims of a hallucination last night. Who knows? Maybe they're right."

Dinner progressed uneventfully, but as nine o'clock approached, everyone grew apprehensive. The grandfather clock began chiming out the time. *Bong, bong, bong*, it rang. The guests smiled nervously. *Bong, bong, bong*. One guest poured himself another glass of wine. *Bong, bong, bong* . . . and then it stopped. The room was silent.

Rain lashed at the windows . . . but the French doors did not open and the ghost did not appear.

One of the women guests poked her husband. "I told you, Albert. What happened last night was a hallucination: some weird kind of mass hysteria. My psychiatrist says that happens sometimes."

Everyone seemed relieved.

"I'll have dessert now," Jamie said. "A large slice of black forest cake, please."

"Anything you like," Harold said. He was thrilled they had been spared Saskia's ghostly vengeance. "And free champagne for all my guests," he told the waitress.

The mood in the Dining Hall suddenly lightened.

Then Betsy, the waitress, returned—without the dessert. "Mr. Ferguson," she screamed, "you've got to come to the kitchen. Bridget is terrified. She swears there's a ghost down there—and it's an evil demon, she says."

The guest rose from their seats. "That's it," said one man, "I'm leaving. I'm not paying a hundred dollars a night to be scared to death!"

"Me too," said another.

"We can't leave *now*," said one woman. "It's not safe to drive down the mountain in this storm."

"Maybe you're right," the old man agreed. "Let's all go to our rooms and lock ourselves in. But if anything happens during the night, I'm *suing* you, Mr. Ferguson."

The guests gave Harold a scornful look, then proceeded to their rooms.

Harold looked frazzled. "I guess I'd better get down to the kitchen and investigate this new disaster!"

By the time Harold and the twins arrived in the kitchen, things had settled down. Bridget was seated in a corner by the hearth, sipping a cup of tea.

The manor house kitchen was truly unique, and Amy could see why Bridget was so proud of it. It combined all the best elements of the past and the present. It had huge microwave ovens, dishwashers, and blenders, but it also had beamed ceilings and a giant stone hearth. Shiny copper pots and kettles hung from metal rings above a long butcher-block table.

"We finally got Bridget calmed down," said a waiter, "but she keeps insisting something evil is going on. She's so scared, she can barely talk."

Harold placed his hands on Bridget's shoulders. "What's wrong, old girl?" he asked in his most charming manner.

Bridget sniffed into her tissue. "Oh, Master Harold, it's glad I am to see you. I'll not spend another night in this place—not with that terrible demon."

"You mean Saskia?" Jamie asked. "Did you see her?"

"It's not the lady of the Manor I'm talking about, child.

53

I know how to behave in the presence of ladylike ghosts. Ghosts, like the poor, are always with us. But this thing . . ." Bridget's lips quivered, and her eyes had the frightening glint of terror. "It's like nothing I've ever known. At first, I thought it was a banshee because of the strange things it's been doing. But tonight—well, no banshee ever behaved like that!"

"What's a banshee?" Amy asked.

"You'd better start at the beginning, old girl," Harold suggested, pulling some chairs up to the hearth.

Bridget blew her nose and composed herself. Then she explained: "Banshees are rackety spirits, Miss Amy. Lots of Irish houses have them. They open kitchen drawers, throw lumps of coal, knock pictures off the wall—but there's no great harm in them. My uncle Patty liked to say he lived with two banshees all his life. That was a bit of joke, because one of them was his wife."

Harold was getting impatient. "Get to the point, Bridget."

"Yes, sir. When I first came here a few weeks ago, I noticed things being moved about in my kitchen. The staff all swore they hadn't done it."

"What kinds of things?" Jamie asked.

"My pots, my dishes, my cutlery," Bridget explained. "Everything was in different cupboards. Banshees, I told myself, and thought nothing of it. Then a few days ago I stacked all my copper pots to be cleaned. When I returned, they'd all been polished and hung back on the hooks. But you see, Master Harold, banshees only *mess* things up—they *never* clean." Bridget leaned over and grabbed Harold's hand, as if to punctuate her observation. "It was then I decided it must be the wee folk here in my kitchen."

"The *wee* folk?" Amy asked.

"Yes, the wee folk will often do a kindly deed; they're very *friendly* spirits."

Despite Bridget's distress, Harold could not restrain his amusement. "But now you don't think it's the wee folk?"

"Oh, no, sir; it's definitely not the wee folk. It's a demon, it is, for sure. I swear on the graves of all my dear departed. And I'll not be sharing my kitchen with a demon."

"Hold on," Harold said. "If there *is* a ghost here, which I doubt, it's probably Saskia Vandermeer. She's probably—well, overseeing things."

Bridget stared at her employer as if he were insane. "Don't be silly, sir. What would a fine lady the likes of her be doing scrubbing my pots for me? That's foolish. No, sir, after tonight, I know it's a wicked evil spirit that's loose among us."

"Why?" Jamie asked. "What happened tonight?"

Trembling, Bridget raised her hand and pointed toward the hearth. "It's still there, look for yourself."

Harold glanced down at the stone floor of the hearth. There, lettered in ashes, was the word *MURDER.*

"Don't bother to sweep it away," Bridget said. "Every time I do, it comes right back again."

"That's ridiculous," Harold said, then he took a brush and swept the ashes aside. As he replaced the brush on its hook, a chill wind swept through the kitchen, and the ashes re-formed their terrible message on the hearth: *MURDER*.

"You see," said Bridget, trembling. "I told you. It's an evil demon, it is; and that's not the worst of it. Go look in the microwave oven."

"The what?"

"Go ahead and look in it, sir," she said, covering her face with her hands. "I keep praying it's not still there, but I know it is."

The twins glanced at each other, both trying to imagine what horrid thing "it" might be.

Boldly Harold walked toward the microwave oven and opened the door.

Inside was a large pile of *snow*.

"It's against the laws of nature," cried Bridget, "that's what it is. This house has unleashed some terrible force, and none of us are safe in our beds!"

Chapter Nine

BRIDGET, THE ONLY STAFF MEMBER WHO LIVED AT THE MANOR, refused to spend another night there. Despite the storm, she insisted Harold drive her down the mountain to the lodge, and reluctantly he agreed. The other employees refused to work the night shift and went home. The guests, afraid to leave their rooms, locked themselves in and prayed for morning to arrive quickly.

The sudden lack of room service annoyed Jamie. He had, after all, planned to order a late-night snack. And now it was almost midnight, and the storm had grown worse. Harold had not returned, and the phone lines were down.

"The roads must be flooded," Jamie said. "Uncle Harry is probably spending the night in town, so I guess we should go to bed."

But Amy was overwhelmed with sadness as she pondered the tragic presence in the Manor. "I'm going back down to the kitchen," she said.

"Are you crazy? Look, I was kidding about a midnight snack. Forget it."

"I can't forget what Jeb said," she explained. Some irresistible force seemed to compel Amy to return downstairs. "I must go, Jamie."

"Okay, then I'll go with you."

The Great Hall of the Manor was dark and deserted. Outside, the wind moaned through the trees, and heavy branches pressed against the windows, as if attempting to stare inside. The grandfather clock rang out a dozen deafening chimes.

As the twins proceeded down the stairs toward the kitchen, Jamie shivered and pulled his robe tighter. "Why's it so cold down here?"

Amy felt the cold, too, and knew it was an unearthly chill. She approached the heavy oak doors of the kitchen and pushed them open. The hearth, which Uncle Harold had dampened hours earlier, was now ablaze.

"Who could've lit that up again?" Jamie asked, peeking in the door.

Amy proceeded inside. The crackling fire did nothing to warm the interior. It was so unbearably frigid, Amy's breath immediately turned to damp vapor before her eyes. Jamie gasped when he saw the reason why. One wall of the kitchen was a frozen block of ice! The sinks and cupboards were all frozen solid, and icicles hung from the wooden beams.

Time had been frozen as well. All the modern appliances were buried beneath the frost. All that remained visible within the kitchen were the utensils of a bygone era.

"Don't come in," Amy cautioned. "Stay back, Jamie, there's a powerful force in here."

"I'm not blind." Jamie proceeded through the doorway. Looking around for a weapon, he spotted a meat cleaver lying beside the dirty pots and pans on the butcher-block table. "Whatever it is, I'm ready for it," he said, brandishing the chopper.

Amy felt herself under attack—an attack of sensations both sad and terrifying. Alien emotions were being channeled through her body. As Jamie stood guard with the meat cleaver, she crept toward the hearth. It was from there she sensed the vibrations emanating.

And it was there that Amy saw the figure veiled in a filmy mist—a pathetically thin figure huddled against the hearth, shivering. A young girl about Amy's age, she had reddish-brown skin, which the cold had tinged with blue. Her deerskin moccasins were ripped and shredded, and frostbite covered her exposed feet. The girl's head was bent, and she held her knees close to her in a vain effort to keep warm. She wore a soiled, tattered deerskin dress with wampum decorating its fringes. Her light brown hair was plaited into a long braid.

Trembling, the apparition looked up and stared at Amy. There was a haunting, pleading expression in the girl's bright blue eyes.

"Who are you?" Amy whispered.

59

The girl recoiled as if in terror. Huddling closer to the hearth, she whimpered softly.

"I won't hurt you," Amy said, and reached out her hand in a gesture of friendship.

Seeing this, the girl's face softened, and she made an attempt to extend her frozen, trembling hand in return. But as she did so, icicles formed in the space between both their fingertips.

"I've come to help you," Amy explained. "*Can* I help you? What do you want here?"

The girl stared in silence, her pale eyes filled with fear.

Despite her costume, the girl looked nothing like an Indian. "Where are you from?" Amy asked. "Are you Indian?"

The girl's body began to shiver uncontrollably. She opened her mouth and emitted a frightening scream, more like the sound of a wounded animal caught in a trap. "*Creecreecreecreecree!*" she wailed.

It was the most pitiful cry Amy had ever heard, the sound of a soul in torment. The girl crouched by the fire, but it could yield no warmth to her frozen body.

"Are you Indian?" Amy repeated the question. "What are you doing here? What are you afraid of?"

The spirit repeated the terrifying sound. "*Creecreecreecreecree.*" And then she uttered a long chain of equally incomprehensible words: "Baffin—baffin—lomles—lomles—overfall—will not pledge—will not."

Amy drew closer. "I don't understand. What do you want?" she said pleadingly.

Jamie was still in the doorway, the meat cleaver poised

above his head. "What's going on? Who are you talking to?"

"There's a spirit by the hearth, Jamie. It's a young girl dressed like an Indian, and she's terribly frightened."

"That makes two of us," Jamie said, staring toward the hearth. All he could see was another wall of ice beginning to form beside the fire.

Then total fear enveloped the apparition. Gripped by a terrifying vision, she stared past Amy and began to shriek. "Sheshesheshesheshe!"

Amy quickly glanced around to see what had frightened the girl so. The ghost of Saskia Vandermeer had begun to materialize through the wall. Her face was taut with unyielding anger. In her hands she carried a spherical object which radiated light. "Liar!" she shouted. "Wretched liar. The busybody had revealed you for what you are!"

For a moment Amy stood rooted to the ground, unable to move. She felt locked between two opposing forces, each one magnetized and pulling her in opposite directions.

Saskia approached the apparition huddled beside the fire. "There is no refuge for you here," she cried. Her voice was coarse and guttural; it bristled with hatred. "You must be cast out as the half-caste that you are." She laughed maniacally. "Cast out, I say. Doomed *forever!*"

Saskia's ghost drew closer to the frightened child. She towered over her, a pitiless expression on her cold, hard face. She laughed again, then vanished into the fire of the hearth. The small huddled figure trembled. Tears fell from the girl's eyes, and each teardrop transformed itself into an icy crystal. Frost now covered the entire hearth, yet the fire still burned within. With a sob the wretched child then vanished as well.

Amy stood motionless. Shivers ran through her body, but these were not shivers brought on by the cold. They were chills of recognition. Amy realized the tormented drama she had just witnessed had been played out hundreds of times before. It was a drama that would continue to occur *eternally*, unless the anguish within the child's heart could somehow be laid to rest.

"C'mon, Jamie," she whispered, "let's get out of here. We have to figure out a way to help that poor girl, but I don't know how!"

Chapter Ten

AS THE TWINS HURRIED BACK UPSTAIRS, THE GRANDFATHER clock sounded a single chime. When they had safely returned to Amy's room, they switched on every light they could find.

Seated on the floor with a pad and pencil, Jamie wrote down everything his sister could remember. He stared at the words he'd scribbled on the pad: "baffin," "lomles," "overfall," "will not pledge." He frowned.

"I told you it was gibberish," Amy said. "It makes no sense at all. How can we help this ghost if we can't understand her?"

"It must have a meaning," Jamie insisted. "Did you say she was Indian? American or East Indian?"

"American; at least she was dressed like one. But she didn't look Indian at all."

"A costume, maybe?" Jamie suggested.

"Perhaps. But why would she be in costume?"

"I don't know. Madame Vandermeer gave lots of fancy-dress balls, didn't she? Maybe this girl came dressed as an Indian maiden. While she was at the ball, someone must've *murdered* her."

"Who?" Amy asked. "Madame Vandermeer?"

"Could be. That would explain why the girl is so scared of her."

"But why would someone murder a child? And why was the kitchen frozen?"

"Beats me," Jamie said. "It's like December down there. If those ghosts are powerful enough to change the seasons, we'd better watch our step."

Amy sighed. "If only you'd seen them too. *Everyone* saw Saskia the other night. Why couldn't you see her this time?"

"You're the ghost expert, Amy, not me. Did Saskia look the same as she did when we all saw her?"

"Exactly the same, except for that thing she was carrying."

"What thing?" he asked. "You didn't say she was carrying anything."

"Didn't I? Well, it was sort of like a mirror, I guess. That's when she mentioned the busybody."

"The what?" Jamie quickly wrote that down. "Hey, you've left out lots of stuff."

"Sorry, it's hard to remember it all." Amy thought back, trying to recall the ghost's exact words. "She said, 'The busybody has revealed you for what you are.' "

"Now we're getting somewhere," Jamie said excitedly.

"We are?"

"Well—maybe. That could be a message. Saskia might've been trying to tell us something."

"What?"

Jamie thought a moment. "A busybody is like a gossip, right? Well, maybe someone in town knows something about an unsolved murder that happened here at the Manor long ago."

"It would have to be a pretty old someone," Amy noted. "That was two hundred and twenty-five years ago."

"True, but townspeople pass on information like that for generations. It's worth a try."

Amy agreed. It was worth a try.

By early the next morning brilliant sunlight had enveloped the grounds of Vandermeer Manor. Birds sang in the trees, and the sweet aroma of mountain thyme filled the air. There was no evidence of the turbulent storm that had come the night before.

There was also no evidence of the ghostly visitors. As the twins entered the kitchen they noticed everything was back to normal. No cryptic message appeared on the hearth, nor were there remnants of the snow and ice that had encased the room. There was only the warm sweet smell of sunshine pouring through the kitchen windows.

In fact, things were better than normal. Amy quickly noticed that all the dirty pots and pans that Bridget had abandoned the night before were now gleaming on their hooks.

"You suppose Bridget came back?" Amy asked hopefully.

The twins noticed their uncle Harold at the stove frying some eggs. "Bridget has not come back," he announced. "And will not," he added emphatically. "She's still down at the lodge and refuses to set foot in this place. As she puts it, she'd rather live with the devil she knows than the devil she doesn't."

"Then who shined all those pots?" Amy asked. "Was it you, Uncle Harold?"

Harold flipped his eggs, then watched them slide down the side of the stove. "Me? I'm having enough trouble rustling up two lousy eggs. It must've been the 'banshees' or the 'wee folk' or whatever else lives inside this million-dollar nightmare!"

"I'm sorry," Jamie said. "Aren't there any guests left?"

"Not one. When I drove back this morning, they were all gone. I guess you kids had better leave too," he added sadly. "Frankly, I don't believe there's any danger here, but I can't take chances. I know I promised you guys you'd live like kings for a while, but—well, I guess I forgot kings often get *beheaded*."

"We're not leaving," Amy said. "We're going to help you discover what's going on here."

"That's right," Jamie said. "If we figure out what the ghosts want, they'll leave you alone."

"I'm already alone," said Harold gloomily, "and likely to remain so." He threw a copy of the *Hudson Valley*

66

Bulletin on the table. "Once folks read that, I'll *never* get another booking."

The twins read the article written by Mr. Deutch, who had been a guest at the Manor. He ended it by saying: "Rumor has it, the ghost is a hoax. I'm not certain what I saw while at Vandermeer Manor, but take note: despite the impressive restoration and the terrific view, I'd personally spend my vacation elsewhere."

"That does it," said Harold. "Soon the word will be all over four counties and I'll be stuck with this empty white elephant. C'mon, kids, you'd better pack. There's a bus back to Monroe this afternoon."

"We told you we're not leaving," Jamie said. "We're staying to solve this mystery."

"Thanks for the offer, Jamie, but this isn't a game. If something happens here, I don't want you kids around."

"We have a stake in this too," Jamie said. "Dad's money is tied up in this place too."

"Don't hit a guy when he's down," Harold said, obviously offended. "I'll pay Richard back every cent he put into this place, I promise."

"Please let us help," Amy said. "Jeb told us we're supposed to."

"Who's Jeb?"

"I can't tell you."

"With my luck, he's probably another *ghost*," Harold said in jest.

Amy felt forced to lie. "We can't go home now. Mom and Dad are away for the weekend, so we'll have to stay at least until Monday."

Jamie quickly picked up his sister's subterfuge. "That's right. Until Monday at least."

Harold finally gave in. "Okay, but promise me you won't go looking for trouble, because I'm afraid you might find it."

"We won't," Jamie promised. "Right now all we want to find is the local blabbermouth."

Luke MacFee admitted to being eighty-four years old. Folks in town told the twins that meant he was probably only eighty-two. "Up here," explained the druggist, "when folks get past seventy, they add on years instead of taking them off. Age gives a person dignity."

The druggist couldn't attest to Luke's dignity, but he did confirm that Luke had a passel of stories about the old days. "You'll find him in his usual spot on the rocker outside the General Store."

Luke MacFee was seated on the shady side of the porch, beside the nail kegs; he was peeling an apple. Old age had creased his leathery face, but he still had a youthful twinkle in his eye.

"Hi, Mr. MacFee," Jamie said. "We hear you've got lots of good old stories to tell."

"That's the truth," he said with a smile that revealed a mouth without teeth. "Only nowadays folks rarely come to listen. They're all too busy at home with their VCRs. Time was, on a Saturday I'd have a whole porchful of kids your age sitting around listening to the old tales. No one comes now," he said wistfully. "Times change. I figure to get myself a VCR one of these days—see what all the fuss is about."

As Luke slowly rocked back and forth, a young woman came out of the General Store carrying an old flour tin. "This will make a marvelous lamp," she said, displaying it proudly. She packed it into the trunk of her car and rode off.

Luke chuckled. "Typical. City folks are always scouting around up here looking for treasures. They're always looking to turn something into something when it already *is* something."

"*We'd* like to hear a story," said Amy.

"You would?" he asked in surprise. "How come? No VCR?"

"A scary story," Jamie added. "Do you know about any unsolved murders that happened around her long ago?"

Luke finished peeling his apple in one complete swirl, then threw the skin in the trash bucket. He cut the fruit into four sections and offered some to the twins. "Unsolved murders, eh? Sure, we had a mystery up here once, long ago."

"A murder?" Jamie asked hopefully. "Are you sure it was a murder?"

Luke slowly gummed his apple. "There's not much in life folks can be sure of, son; that's what makes it worth living. But murder is a definite certainty."

"Was it an unsolved murder?" Jamie asked.

"To this day."

Jamie took out the notes he had written down the

night before. "Was the dead person's name Baffin—or Lomles?"

"Nope," said Luke. "Zack Moody was his name, though folks always called him Old Gray Moody because of his long gray beard."

"Are you sure it wasn't Baffin or Lomles?" Jamie asked again, this time disappointedly.

"Come to think of it," Luke said, "it could've been— seeing as how no one was ever rightly certain who murdered who."

"Please tell us about it," Amy said eagerly.

Luke pointed beyond the valley. "Long time ago, Old Gray Moody had a cabin up in those woods. He was a trapper and hunter who came into town to sell his skins— beavers and deer, mostly." He paused a moment to make sure he had the twins' full attention. Like all good story-tellers, Luke chose his words carefully for their dramatic effect. "No one liked Old Gray Moody much; no sir. Folks said he took too much pleasure in his killing. And folks didn't much like the fact that he always carried his hatchet with him. He wore it strung around his waist on a belt. Yes sir, there's no denying Moody was a surly sort without a friend in the world. Rumor had it he'd buried some treasure up there by his cabin. Old Moody never denied it, but he said if anyone came snooping around after it, he'd chop their head off." Luke glanced at the twins out of the corner of his eye. They were still listen-ing intently, so he continued. "It was on a September the fifteenth, folks say. Old Gray Moody came into town. He stopped at the local saloon and had a few too many. As

70

usual, he bragged he had a king's ransom buried up in those woods. He warned if anyone came sniffing around, he'd chop them up on sight. Well sir, months went by and no one saw Zack Moody after that—not a soul. He'd run up a big bill in town and folks wanted their money, so some of them set up into the woods to find him. They found him, all right—at least folks thought it was him. Hard to tell, though, seeing as how he had no head. It'd been cut clean off, you see—clean as a whistle and never found. Moody's hatchet was wedged into a tree stump, fresh blood still on it. As folks around here used to tell it, if you go up in those woods you'll still see that hatchet stuck in that stump—and it'll still have fresh blood on it. As for Moody's head, it was never found, and neither was the treasure he loved to brag about. Of course, the body may've been Moody's victim—someone who'd tried to get their hands on his treasure. No one ever knew for sure. But those fool enough to go into those woods can see that hatchet to this day—still moist with the blood of Old Gray Moody, or someone, so folks used to say." Luke paused, closed his paring knife, and slipped it into his pocket. "What d'ya think, isn't that a corker of a story? I'll bet it beats them chop-'em-ups you watch on your VCR."

The twins had become so involved in the story, they hadn't realized it had no relevance. "Yeah, that was scary," Jamie said, "but it has nothing to do with Vandermeer Manor."

"Who said it did?"

"We were hoping you'd know about an unsolved murder up at the Manor," Amy explained.

"That place? It hasn't been lived in for years. I hear tell some fool millionaire bought it. Guess he figures to make something out of something that used to be something—just like all those rich city folks."

"Don't you know anything about a girl who might've been murdered up there?" Amy asked. "We think she might've been Indian."

"Indian?" Luke shrugged and shook his head. "*Town* stories are my line," he explained. "If you're looking for stories about Indians, you'd best go see Cliff Hightower. He knows all the old tales—been collecting them since he was a boy. I think he's got some idea to put them into a book someday."

"Thanks for your time, Mr. MacFee," Amy said.

Luke yawned and stretched, then resumed rocking. "No trouble, kids, come around again. Long stories, short stories—you name it, I'll tell it. I've got a doozy about Mrs. Murdock's well. Bet you can't guess what she had buried down there for twenty-seven years."

"Another time," Jamie said. "Thanks again."

Chapter Eleven

THE INDIAN TRAIL SOUVENIR SHOP WAS IN THE CENTER OF town. A large wooden cigar-store Indian stood at the entrance. The bell above the shop door jingled as the twins entered.

"Be right with you," called a voice from the back room.

Jamie couldn't wait to see what Cliff Hightower looked like, so took little notice of the feathered headdresses, moccasins, toy tepees, colorful beads, maps of old Indian trails, and various other touristy collectibles on display in the shop. He had assumed Cliff would be a stately old Indian wrapped in a handwoven blanket, but he was wrong. A handsome young man wearing designer jeans and an MIT sweatshirt came from the back room. "What can I do for you?" he asked.

"We haven't come to buy anything," Amy said.

"Browsers are welcome," Cliff said, smiling. "Shout if you want help; I'll be in back."

"We do want help," Jamie said. "We'd like information. Mr. MacFee said you know lots of old Indian legends."

Cliff Hightower laughed. "MacFee? He's some character, isn't he? When I was little, he scared me to death with his story about Old Gray Moody. For years I was too frightened to walk in the woods."

"Is it really true?" Jamie asked. "Did you ever see the hatchet?"

"I never did and I'm sure I never will. But don't tell Luke that; it would spoil all his fun. He's made quite a career out of scaring the kids who come up here. Luke is known as our local color." Cliff came around the counter and went to the bookcase. "You say you're interested in Indian legends? What tribe? I've several books here which might interest you. Indian myths are very varied."

"We don't know what tribe," Jamie said. "We don't even know if this girl was an Indian."

"What girl?" Cliff asked.

"We don't know that, either," Amy said, "but we think there may've been an Indian girl living at Vandermeer Manor long ago. And we think she may've been murdered."

Cliff stared at the children with interest. "You kids aren't talking about myth—that's history."

"You mean it really happened?" Jamie asked. "Was her name Baffin or Lomles?"

"No," Cliff said, "her name was Turtledove. She was

actually only half Indian—half-caste they called it in those days."

Amy remembered hearing Saskia's ghost use that word. "A *half-caste*, that's right," she said excitedly. "Then you know about her. Was she really murdered?"

"Oh, it was murder," said Cliff, "though no one called it that. It's very odd *you* know about her. I've been collecting historical data about the Indian presence in this area for years. Once I finish college, I hope I'll have time to write it all down. My great-great-aunt in Albany who died several years ago told me about Turtledove. Her great-great-grandmother had told her the story. So how on earth could you kids know about her? The story is over two hundred years old. It's one of those incidents no one even knows or cares about."

"*We* care," said Amy. "Please tell us everything."

Cliff studied the twins, puzzled and intrigued by their interest. "Everything? That'll take some time. You'd better come in back with me; I was just about to have lunch. Care for some herbal tea and cheese?"

"First of all," Cliff said as the twins munched on cheese and sipped rose-hip tea, "let me ask you how much you know about the patroonships which used to exist in the Hudson River valley."

"Not much," Jamie said. "Our uncle told us patroons were like feudal lords."

"That's right," said Cliff. "I hope you don't mind a little history lesson—it'll help explain things."

75

"Oh, we're used to history lessons," Amy said. "Our dad is a history professor."

"Well," Cliff began, "these are the basic historical facts. Originally, Henry Hudson explored this area for the Dutch East India Company. He bought the land from the Indians, and that gave the Dutch their claim to the region. But in order to ensure that Dutch would settle in this new land, Holland granted wealthy landowners large estates. These landowners, called patroons, controlled the land and all the people on it. The original patroon, Kiliaen Vandermeer, owned thousands of acres. Jan Vandermeer was his direct descendant. His word was law. He could bring people to trial, execute them, and he could exact payment from all his tenants in money, goods, and services. Vandermeer owned everything and everyone. The expenses of the tenant farmers on his estate were so great, they were bound into his service for life. In addition, once a year they had to pledge an oath of allegiance to him."

Amy suddenly remembered something the girl's spirit had cried out: "will not pledge—will not."

Cliff glanced at her. "Is this story too boring?"

"No," she said, "please go on."

"Okay," Cliff said, and took a sip of his tea. "The Vandermeers had hundreds of tenants and servants on their estate. One of them was this half-caste Indian girl. No one knew where she came from, how she got there, or what tribe she belonged to. As the story goes, she worked in the kitchen of the Manor."

"Polishing the copper pots?" Amy asked.

"That's right," Cliff said, surprised. "How'd you know that?"

"A lucky guess," Amy said. "Go on."

"The other servants didn't like her much. In fact, most of them thought she was crazy."

"Why?"

"When the girl first arrived at the Manor, she was about eleven years old. She refused to tell anyone her name—said she didn't have one yet. About a year later she informed the servants her name was Turtledove because that name had been revealed to her in her dreams. Well, the servants knew nothing about Indian culture, so they thought that was strange."

"Sounds peculiar to me too," Jamie said. "How can you receive a name in your dreams?"

"It's part of Indian religion," Cliff explained. "You see, Indians believed that their dream life, known as the dream time, was as real as their waking life. When a child came of age, he or she would fast several days and ponder the visions that appeared in dreams. This is how people selected the personal manitou who would be their guardian."

"What's a manitou?" Amy asked.

"It's a guardian spirit," Cliff explained. "Most manitous are animals: bears, falcons, crows, ducks. Then, of course, there is the Great Manitou who is the God spirit who governs all things. He's called Kitchi Manitou."

Jamie had figured things out. "You mean the girl dreamed of a turtledove, so she named herself that?"

"Exactly," Cliff said. "One's personal manitou was usually evoked in song. Anyway, that's probably how she decided on the name Turtledove."

"That doesn't sound crazy," Amy said.

"Maybe not, but Turtledove said lots of other strange things. She insisted the Vandermeers didn't actually own the land. Turtledove said *she* owned it and that it was part of her rightful heritage."

"Maybe she was right," Jamie said. "After all, Indians originally owned this land."

"That's true," Cliff said, "but the Indian concept of ownership is quite different. They believe no one can truly own the land. They feel it's peopled with many spirits and is part of the supernatural power which emanates from all things. There are sun, moon, water, tree, and earth spirits, so no human truly owns anything. Besides, Turtledove insisted she wasn't a member of any tribe which settled this area."

"What tribe was she from?" Jamie asked.

"Turtledove kept that a secret. She never told anyone. She'd only say her people came from far away. She vowed that someday she would prove her heritage and cast out the lady of the Manor. So you see why everyone thought she was crazy. Turtledove was a lowly servant girl, probably an orphan, so everyone laughed at her grand ideas. Everyone but Madame Vandermeer, who refused to put up with insolence from her servants. When the day came for everyone to officially pledge their yearly oath to the patroon, Turtledove refused. Madame Vandermeer ordered her punished with a beating, but that didn't deter the child. Worse punishment came when Madame

Vandermeer accused her of trying to take something from her bedroom. Kitchen servants were never allowed near the bedrooms, but Madame Vandermeer found Turtledove in her private quarters, stealing something."

"What did she steal?" Amy asked.

"My great-great-aunt wasn't certain, but she knew it wasn't jewelry or fancy clothes. It was either a picture or a map—something of little value."

"Then why did she try to steal it?" Jamie asked.

"No one knew. Somehow, Turtledove felt it important she take it. Anyway, Madame Vandermeer caught her in the act. She was furious. She ordered the girl out of the house. It was a freezing cold night in the middle of December, and there was a snowstorm. Madame Vandermeer ordered her servants to lock the kitchen door and not let the child back inside until morning. Poor Turtledove had nothing to protect her from the cruel weather."

"Only a deerskin dress and moccasins," Amy interjected.

Cliff looked puzzled. "How'd you know that?"

"Another lucky guess," Jamie said. "Don't stop, tell us the rest."

"Well, ordering the child to spend the night outdoors was like delivering her death sentence. Snow fell all night, and by morning the grounds were frozen solid. The other servants had been too frightened to go against Madame Vandermeer's orders. When they found Turtledove the next morning, she was suffering from frostbite and near death. They brought her into the kitchen and laid her beside the hearth, but it was too late. A few hours later she was dead."

"That's terrible," Jamie said. "Madame Vandermeer *murdered* that girl."

Cliff nodded. "But no one really cared. Turtledove was a half-caste, half-crazed servant, so no one cared." He sipped the remainder of his tea. "Well, that's about it, kids."

"That can't be all," Amy said. "Why did Turtledove think she owned the land? Who were her people? Where did she come from? What did she try to steal? Why is she haun— I mean, there must be more to the story."

"Sure there is," Cliff said, "but no one knows it. It's buried in the past—forgotten forever."

"I guess you're right," Jamie said. Discovering who the mysterious ghost was did not seem to solve anything. The mystery surrounding Turtledove was more confusing than ever.

"But it can't be forgotten forever," Amy said. That would mean Turtledove would be *lost* forever—somewhere between life and death, never knowing peace.

"Sorry, kids," Cliff said, "that's all I know."

Chapter Twelve

"I WISH WE COULD DO SOMETHING," JAMIE SAID. "POOR TUR-tledove's ghost keeps freezing to death in the kitchen every night. I mean—"

"I know what you mean," Amy replied. "It's just like Jeb said—her spirit is caught in a life-death cycle."

"And she has to share the house with her *murderer*. What a rotten deal."

It took nearly an hour for the twins to return to the Manor. Their walk was spent reviewing the clues both ghosts had given them. They were convinced the message was important, but still couldn't make sense of it.

"I wish we knew what Turtledove tried to steal from Madame Vandermeer's bedroom," Jamie said. "I'll bet that's the key to the mystery."

When they arrived back at the Manor, their uncle Harold was on the phone in the Main Hall. He looked exhausted and frazzled. "No, Jerry," he argued, "I can't afford to put another dime into this place. It's become an albatross around my neck! . . . Well, I'll have to live without the gold sconces. . . . Yes, and the bust of Plato. . . . Okay, they're authentic, who cares? Ghosts are authentic, too, but who needs them." He slammed down the phone. "Hi, kids, did you have a good time in town?"

"It was interesting," Jamie said. "It's possible there's a ghost in the kitchen who thinks this land belongs to her."

"If she pays the bills, she can have it," Harold said disgustedly. "This place has eaten up money like a monster. That was my very expensive decorator on the phone. He insists I need to install tons more junk from the original design of the house: sconces, statues, and more busybodies in the master bedrooms."

"More *what*?" Jamie asked.

"It's ridiculous," Harold said angrily. "I don't have one guest, so why do I need more sconces and busybodies?"

"What are busybodies?" Amy asked eagerly.

"Those mirrored things," Harold explained. "I've already got one in the master bedroom in the West Wing."

"Wasn't that originally Saskia Vandermeer's bedroom?" Jamie asked.

"Right," Harold said, "but I don't need any more."

"Show us where it is," Amy said excitedly.

"Where what is?"

"The *busybody*, Uncle Harold. Show us!"

The twins pulled on their uncle's arm, insisting he take them upstairs to the West Wing.

"Okay," he said, "what's the big interest?"

Harold led the way to the third floor, then down the corridor to the largest bedroom in the Manor. "I was hoping this could be the Executive Suite," he explained, opening the door. Plush Persian rugs covered the parquet floor. In the center of the room was a mahogany four-poster with intricate carving. Thick brocaded drapes covered the huge windows, and portraits and maps hung in gilt frames on the damask-covered walls.

"Where's the busybody?" Amy asked.

"Up there." Harold pointed to a spot above the center window. A set of three circular mirrors hung above the molding, enabling a person to view the interior of the room while standing in the doorway. "Look around if you like," he said. "I'm calling Jerry back to make sure he doesn't put me in the poorhouse. I'll get there soon enough on my own!"

As Harold left, Amy glanced up at the busybody. "Yes, that's what Saskia was carrying last night. What's it mean, Jamie?"

"It means we're getting warmer. Amy, let's try an experiment. Walk down the hall a bit and then turn around and walk back toward this room. When you pass by, look up at the busybody and tell me what you see."

Amy did as instructed. Walking by the room, she glanced up at the mirror and saw the wall facing north. "I see the wall with the map hanging on it."

"That's it," said Jamie excitedly. "Cliff said Turtledove

may have been trying to steal a map from this room. Madame Vandermeer must've passed by and caught her in the act."

"Why would she want a map?"

"I don't know. Harold said this room has been reproduced exactly, so let's see."

The twins hurried to the north wall and took down the frame. It was a map of Hudson Strait and Hudson Bay, including the areas north of Quebec. The inscription at the bottom read: "This illustrates Henry Hudson's fourth and last voyage." Several landmasses were noted in script: Furious Overfall, Baffin Island, and Lomles Inlet.

"Those are the words Turtledove cried out," Amy said. "This was the map she tried to steal! But why? Why would a servant girl want a map of Henry Hudson's last voyage?"

Jamie sighed. "I don't know. Every clue makes things more confusing. What could Turtledove have to do with Henry Hudson? They didn't even live in the same century."

"There must be some connection," Amy said. "Do you know anything about Henry Hudson?"

"Not much," Jamie said. "He explored this area, so they named the Hudson River after him. He explored up in Canada, so they named Hudson Bay after him. What else is there to know?"

"Maybe Dad can tell us," Amy said. "Let's call home and find out."

"Hi, Mom," Amy said. "How are things?"

"Quiet, dear; very quiet," said Miriam Ferguson. "How are things up there? Your dad and I were wondering when you'd call us."

"Well, we've been real busy; you know how it is."

"Of course. Are you both having a good time? Do you have a nice suntan?"

"Listen, Mom, could you put Dad on the phone? Jamie needs to talk to him."

Mrs. Ferguson seemed concerned. "Oh? Is everything all right? Where's your uncle Harold?"

"Things are fine, Mom. Jamie wants to ask Dad something about Henry Hudson."

"Henry who?"

"Hudson, Mom. Henry Hudson."

There was a pause while Amy handed the phone to her brother.

"Hi, Dad. How are things?"

"Quiet, Son; very quiet. How are things up there?"

"Great, really terrific. What can you tell me about Henry Hudson?"

"Henry who?"

"Hudson, Dad. Henry Hudson."

Another pause. "Are you sure everything's okay up there, Jamie?"

"Couldn't be better, Dad. So tell me about Henry Hudson."

"Are you kids playing some kind of trivia game?"

"That's it, Dad—trivia. Do you know some trivia about Henry Hudson?"

"I know some facts, but I wouldn't call them trivial."

"Well, what are they?" Jamie asked impatiently. "When did he discover Hudson Bay?"

"In 1610. Hudson was still looking for the Northwest Passage, only this time he'd been financed by the English, not the Dutch."

"Uh-huh. Go on."

"That's about it. He never returned from that journey. Hudson's crew mutinied. They set Hudson, his son, and seven other crew members adrift in a small boat, without food or water. They were never seen again."

"His crew *mutinied*?"

"That's right," said Mr. Ferguson. "So who wins the game—you or Amy?"

"The what? Oh, the *game*. I don't know yet, Dad. Thanks for the information."

The twins spent the rest of the afternoon reviewing their clues. "It doesn't add up," Jamie said. "Henry Hudson died up in Canada in 1611, but the Vandermeers lived here in the 1760s. Where's the connection?"

Amy sighed. "There is none. One murder has nothing to do with the other."

Something clicked for Jamie. "Yeah, they were both murdered, weren't they? Do you think Turtledove was trying to tell us about Henry Hudson's murder, not her own?"

"Why should she? How could she have known about it? She was an uneducated servant girl, so I doubt if she knew much history."

"True," Jamie said, "but there are different kinds of

history. Some is passed down through generations, like the oral history Cliff collects. He said Turtledove insisted she came from far away, right? Well, what if her people came from Canada? They may've told her the story of Henry Hudson being set adrift."

"What if they did? I still don't see the connection."

"Neither do I," Jamie grumbled. "Let's call Dad again."

"Hi, Dad," Jamie said brightly. "We've got a few more questions about Henry Hudson."

"This game is longer than Monopoly. Well, fire away."

"When Henry Hudson's crew set him adrift, did he drown?"

"Maybe. I guess he drowned or starved or froze to death," Mr. Ferguson explained. "Hudson's boat was set adrift on an ice floe. The Prince of Wales sent ships out to retrieve the bodies, but nothing was ever found. The whole thing is a mystery. We don't even know if the mutineers went to the gallows. They were brought to trial, but there's no record of the verdict. In fact, the record is totally unfinished and has been for three hundred and fifty years."

Jamie's mind raced toward a possible conclusion. "Then Hudson might've *survived*?"

"It's possible," said his father. "The Hudson's Bay Company was established by a group of English businessmen to obtain furs in North America. In 1725 an agent of the company reported that he had traded with an Indian who had surprisingly pale skin. The Indian

87

told him one of his ancestors was an Englishman who had lived in the forest."

"No kidding, Dad. What was the Indian's name?"

"I don't know. He was the last survivor of his tribe, so he'd joined with a tribe in Canada and had become one of them."

Jamie was so excited, he nearly dropped the phone. "A tribe of Indians in Canada? Do you know what tribe, Dad; it's very important."

"Yes, they were Cree Indians."

"Cree Indians?" Jamie repeated. "Did you say *Cree*?"

Amy grew excited too. "That's the word Turtledove kept saying. I thought it was a cry, but it's a word. Maybe she was telling us *she's* a Cree Indian!"

Jamie nodded. "Listen, Dad, thanks a million."

"You're welcome. I don't know what this game's called, but *I'd* like to play it sometime too."

"Sure, Dad. Bye now."

"Wait, your mother wants me to remind you guys to wash out your socks!"

"Sure, Dad; right away. Good-bye."

Jamie hung up the phone and began pacing the room. "Things are falling into place now, Amy. I'll bet Henry Hudson survived that mutiny. Maybe his crew came ashore in the place called Baffin Island. Their boat was probably destroyed, so they had no way of returning to civilization. They could've been adopted by a tribe of Indians. History can't prove otherwise, so it might've happened that way."

"Sure," Amy said, "that's possible."

"We're finally getting somewhere," Jamie said proudly.

"We are? I still don't see the connection between Hudson and Turtledove."

"Use your imagination, Amy. Dad told us Henry Hudson's *son* was set adrift with him. What if his son married one of the Indian maidens from the tribe that rescued them? That would make Turtledove a direct descendant of Henry Hudson!"

"I guess so."

"And that would give Turtledove every reason to believe she had claims on this land. Just imagine it: a poor servant girl who scrubbed pots in Madame Vandermeer's kitchen but knew she had more right to this land than the lady of the Manor."

Amy sensed her brother's suppositions were correct. "I think you're right, Jamie. I'll bet Turtledove is trapped here until someone discovers her secret heritage. And I think we have. I guess we've got to tell her that before she can pass on."

"Do you think she'll appear in the kitchen again tonight?"

"I don't know," Amy said, "we'll have to wait and see."

That evening the twins prepared a simple dinner and served it on the veranda.

Uncle Harold didn't have much of an appetite. "Don't take it personally, this omelet is great. If either of you wants a full-time job as cook, you've got it."

"Cheer up," Jamie said, "I'll bet the staff returns soon. They got frightened, but they'll get over it."

"How come you kids aren't frightened?" Harold asked. "You act as if you've had *experience* with ghosts."

Amy nearly choked on her omelet. The last thing she wanted was for Harold to discover her psychic abilities. "I thought you didn't *believe* in ghosts," she said evasively.

"Of course I don't. I'm sure there's a logical explanation for what's going on here—a magnetic field or something scientific like that. Trouble is, I can't think what it might be."

"Don't bother," Jamie said, "it'll probably all blow over soon, anyway."

Chapter Thirteen

THE TWINS WAITED UNTIL HAROLD WAS ASLEEP. AS THE CLOCK chimed midnight they slowly tiptoed down the hall.

Jamie felt confident the haunting would soon end, which meant the staff would return, and he could once again enjoy the life of a king, at least for the remainder of his vacation. "This hasn't been so hard, after all," he whispered. "Once Turtledove learns we know her secret, she can pass on. Then Madame Vandermeer won't have anyone to bully around anymore and she'll leave too."

"I hope you're right," Amy said as she approached the kitchen door. With some trepidation she turned the knob and pushed the door open.

Jamie, close behind her, switched on the light. The kitchen was immaculate. The copper pots gleamed, the hearth had been scrubbed clean, and every utensil was in its proper place. And there was not one drop of snow or ice anywhere.

As Amy stood in the doorway glancing around, she had no psychic sensations. "I guess the spirits aren't here tonight."

"Not here?" Jamie said disappointedly. "Where'd they go? They have to be here, we have to tell Turtledove we know her secret, and clear up this whole mess."

"Sorry, Jamie, I don't sense anything in the air."

But suddenly a sweet aroma wafted through the room. Amy sniffed the air. It was an incredibly enticing scent, as if all nature had burst into full bloom. "What's that?" she asked.

"Lilacs, I think," Jamie said. "Or is it roses? Whatever it is, it smells great."

Amy pointed toward the window. "Look out there." The lights from the kitchen balcony illuminated the darkness outside. There, the lilac trees and rosebushes, which had lost their flowers a month earlier, were in full bloom again. A misty breeze carried their heady sweetness through the window.

And then the vaporous spirit of Saskia Vandermeer began to materialize. Her delicately chiseled face was pristinely white and luminescent. Fresh spring flowers garlanded her hair, and in her arms she carried fragrant and colorful bouquets. Light rippled against the folds of her blue satin dress, like the sun radiating beneath clear blue water.

"It's Saskia," said Amy. "Can you see her?"

"Sure I can," said Jamie. "She looks gorgeous!"

And so she did. Saskia Vandermeer seemed more than merely beautiful: she was the essence of beauty itself. Madame Vandermeer selected one white rose from her bouquet and extended it toward Amy.

At first Amy was enticed by the spirit's great beauty. She extended her hand toward the single, perfect, thornless flower. But as she did, a wave of psychic recognition swept over her. Suddenly Amy knew her eyes were deceiving her other senses. Saskia Vandermeer was not what she appeared to be. Jebediah's warning flashed through Amy's mind: An impure spirit may assume many masks in order to deceive.

"No," said Amy, backing away, "you're not what you seem to be."

The bouquet Saskia carried began to crumble and turn to dust. The sweet scent of flowers was quickly replaced by the moldy, rank odor of decay. Instantly the rose withered in Saskia's hand, and blood-tipped thorns sprouted along its stem.

Saskia's mask of beauty became a hideous ugliness. "Each thorn shall pierce your heart!" she screamed. "No one intrudes on my domain!"

Jamie stood motionless, transfixed by the spirit's sudden transformation. No vision, actual or imagined, could surpass the horror of Saskia's face. Her melting, rotting flesh hung from charred bones. She held out her decomposing skeletal arms and beckoned Jamie toward her.

Jamie was repelled by the vision yet drawn toward it.

"No," Amy shouted, "don't look at her. She has no power if you don't look at her!"

Saskia's voice crackled with guttural laughter. "No power? I have supreme power!" As she raised her arms above her head, flames shot up from the ground. Fanned by an enormous gust of wind, they leapt up the side of the kitchen wall, consuming everything in their path. Within an instant the kitchen cabinets had blackened with soot.

The twins could feel the heat of the flames racing toward them. Their skin burned and pain shot through their bodies as fire began to creep along their arms.

Amy raced toward the door, grabbed her brother, dragged him outside, then slammed the door behind them. "It's only an illusion," she explained, throwing herself against the closed door and panting for breath. "Keep telling yourself that, Jamie. It's only an illusion as long as we resist. While we have strength she has no power."

Jamie concentrated hard on that thought and felt the burning sensation vanish from his skin. He touched his arms: they were cool and smooth.

"You're right," he said to his sister, "but what got into that ghost? Why's she so mad at us?"

"She knows what we're trying to do," said Amy. "Don't you see? Madame Vandermeer doesn't want us to help Turtledove. She wants the girl to be her servant forever. Now that Saskia's ghost is onto us, we're really in danger!"

In the morning Vandermeer Manor was back to normal. The twins found their uncle Harold in the kitchen cheerfully attempting to mix a bowlful of pancake batter.

"Maybe I forgot the eggs," Harold said, pouring the cementlike substance onto the griddle. "No matter, Bridget will be back tomorrow and I'll be off KP."

The twins stared at the cabinets, which had burst into flame the night before. The china was back in its place on the shelves, unharmed.

"Everyone'll be back soon," Harold announced gaily. "You kids were right. Several of the staff called this morning to apologize for leaving. I guess the storm gave them the heebie-jeebies. I got three new bookings too. Pretty soon this place'll be filled up again."

"People are coming back?" Amy asked. "But they can't; not now."

"No way!" Jamie said. "We've got ourselves a mean dude of a ghost here!"

"What are you babbling about?" Harold asked. "Everything's been fine. Madame Vandermeer's ghost only appeared once, and now she's gone, so there's no harm done. One lousy snowball in the microwave is no big deal."

"*Other* things have been happening, Uncle Harry," said Jamie, "things we haven't told you about."

"Like what?" he asked, flipping a pancake which landed burned-side-up on the griddle.

"Just things," Amy said, tersely, reluctant to reveal the extent of Madame Vandermeer's wrath.

"Nonsense," Harold said, "*I* haven't seen anything. Last night I slept like a baby. Rattling around this big place alone has gotten to you kids."

"No," Jamie said, "there's real danger here. Bridget

was right about that, Uncle Harry. We've got *two* ghosts down in this kitchen. Madame Vandermeer murdered an Indian girl named Turtledove right here, and they both appear at night. Turtledove is covered with frostbite and turns the place into an iceberg. Madame Vandermeer can set the whole joint on fire whenever she likes. First she looks beautiful, then she gets real ugly. She can turn herself into rotting flesh whenever she wants—and she creates a real stink too!"

The smell of burned pancakes began to fill the kitchen. Harold was so distracted, he let them burn a while longer. "Is that so?" he said, dumping the charred disks onto a platter. "Is there anything else I should know?"

"Well," Jamie continued, "the whole deal has something to do with Henry Hudson, but until Turtledove appears again, we can't straighten things out. But the big problem is that Madame Vandermeer doesn't want us talking to Turtledove."

A smile spread across Harold's face, but he tried to suppress it. "Oh, no? Why not?"

"Because of the secret," Jamie explained. "Henry Hudson didn't die up in Canada. At least we don't think so—isn't that right, Amy?"

Amy said nothing. Her uncle didn't believe a word of Jamie's fantastic tale.

"You surprise me, Jamie," Harold said, smothering his burned pancakes with syrup. "Richard always told me Amy was the one with the wild imagination. Anyway, everything's clear to me now. You kids went into town yesterday, didn't you? And you have a nice long talk with Luke MacFee, right? He told you all about Old Gray Moody and that bloody hatchet, didn't he?"

"Sure," Jamie said. "So what?"

Harold laughed. "So *you've* got the heebie-jeebies too! Listen, kids, I don't blame you. If I were your age and heard a story like that, I'd be seeing visions myself. But it's only your imagination. Whatever occurred here is over—finished—got it? Tomorrow the staff returns and it's business as usual. Now, can I interest either of you in one of my cast-iron pancakes?"

Chapter Fourteen

"WE HAVE TO NEUTRALIZE SASKIA'S POWER," AMY SAID.

"Before tomorrow morning when the staff gets back," Jamie added. "But how?"

Amy didn't have the answer. She fixed her gaze on the majestic mountains in the distance and felt helpless. But what was even worse, she felt responsible. Her efforts to aid Turtledove had caused Saskia's uncontrollable anger. "If something awful happens, *I'm* to blame. Do you think it's because I don't know how to use my psychic powers properly?"

"Don't ask me," Jamie said. "You'd better ask J.T. that question."

"Are you sure we should do this?" Amy asked nervously. "What if Uncle Harold comes back?"

"Relax," said Jamie, "Harry'll be in town for hours. His dinner with his accountant will take hours. He's got lots of papers to look over with Mr. Dudley. Besides, what if he does return? No one can see Jeb but you, so c'mon, try to conjure him up. Ask him to neutralize Saskia's power so we can contact Turtledove."

Amy sat on the floor of her room, closed her eyes, then began concentrating all her mental energy toward visualizing the spirit of the lieutenant colonel. But he did not appear. "It's not working."

"Try harder. Jeb has to answer."

Amy tried again. "We need you, Jebediah," she called out, "please appear."

A coolness filled the room, but the spirit did not materialize. Instead, a sudden gust of wind pushed open the balcony doors. The twins felt they might be swept off the floor by its power. Gradually the wind ceased, and the doors slammed shut again.

"Wow," Jamie said, "Jeb arrived with a blast this time!"

"No, Jeb's not here," Amy said. "Something's gone wrong."

After a moment Jebediah Tredwell did begin to materialize beside the balcony doors. "Someone wishes to prevent my appearance, Cousin," he stated. "Some force tries to keep me from you."

"That must be Saskia," Amy said.

"Oh, no," Jamie groaned, "is *she* back again?"

"No, Saskia's not here," Amy explained. "*Jeb* is here."

Jamie glanced around but saw no one. "But you said— Listen, Amy, which ghost is in here with us?"

99

" 'Tis I, James," Jebediah called out. "Take heed; there are many forces at work within this house."

"A mouse?" Jamie asked. "Oh, now I get it. Jeb's here, but I can't understand him, as usual—right?"

Amy nodded. "Listen, Jeb, the ghost of Saskia appeared again. First she looked beautiful, but then she grew ugly and then—"

"You need not elaborate," said Jebediah. "I am aware of the actions of impure spirits. They are unable to maintain a false appearance of beauty, and end by betraying their baser qualities. The lady of the Manor is still cloaked in her corporal vices of cruelty, cupidity, and avarice. She has not risen above them and therefore cannot pass on to a higher plain."

"Does that mean both spirits will be locked within this house forever?" Amy asked.

"Only until they acknowledge the truth of their circumstance. And you have been chosen to guide them toward this goal, my child."

"*Me?*" Amy said. "I *can't*, that's why I called you for help."

"In this endeavor I am unable to assist. These spirits are still cloaked within the elements of their corporal lives and may only be reached on a corporal plain. You and James have done much already. Have you not ascertained the identity of the poor soul doomed to perpetual torment?"

"Yes, her name is Turtledove. We're trying to help her, but Saskia won't let us."

"That's right," Jamie said. "Saskia has put the whammy

on this place. Can't you put the whammy back on her, J.T.? Why can't *you* get rid of her for us?"

Jebediah drew closer. "Such corporal retribution is not appropriate in the spirit world. Spirit is quintessentialized matter, but matter existing in a state which has no analogue within the circle of your comprehension. I fear my powers are not strong enough, and I am not yet purified enough, to effect such a task. As a spirit form, I am still in my infancy."

"What'd he say?" Jamie asked.

Amy shrugged. "He says he can't do it, but I don't understand why."

"Well, someone better do it," Jamie shouted, "or else when Bridget returns to her kitchen she'll have a heart attack! Saskia's ghost is truly gross!"

"Heed me now, Cousins," Jebediah continued, "there is a way by which you may still succeed. You must call upon a spirit of superior elevation. Such a presence will repel the spirit of inferior degree."

"Call *another* spirit?" Amy asked. "From where?"

"The infinitude of space," he replied. "It is filled with spirits in infinite number. Unperceived by you, they are incessantly beside you; for spirits are one of the powers of nature. They are instruments employed, as I am, for the accomplishment of providential design."

"I don't know any other spirits," Amy said, "only you. How do I do it? Who should I call?"

"What's Jeb's advice?" Jamie asked. "To get more ghosts? No way; we've got a bumper crop already!"

Jebediah approached Amy and placed his hands on her

101

shoulders. " 'Tis you who have been chosen for this task, Cousin. Avail yourself of the medianimity within you. Call forth the spirit for whom the tormented child cries out and end the confusion within her soul. Because of her violent end, she clings to her body, for she does not believe herself dead. Help her separate herself from fleshly bonds so she may be reborn into a new existence. For remember, all spirits are eternal."

Slowly the figure of Jebediah Tredwell began to dissolve into particles of light, which floated toward the window and then were gone.

"Well," Jamie asked anxiously, "did Jeb come up with any hot ideas?"

"I'm not sure. He said the whole thing's up to *me*. I'm supposed to contact some other spirit who'll help Turtledove—but I don't know how."

"Maybe he means we should have a *séance*," Jamie suggested. "Isn't that how it's done?"

"I suppose so," said Amy, "but who am I supposed to contact? Jeb didn't tell me that."

"Boy, that guy is really vague sometimes, isn't he?" Jamie chewed on his thumbnail as he walked around the room. "I've got it—Jeb must mean Henry Hudson. After all, he's the only person who might know something about this deal."

"Henry Hudson?"

"Sure. You've got to conjure him up, Amy. Ask him to help us."

Chapter Fifteen

As THE TWINS SAT IN THE KITCHEN, THEY COULD HEAR THE grandfather clock upstairs in the Great Hall chime eight times.

"I feel like a fool," Amy said as she and her brother linked hands across the butcher-block table.

"I know, but this is the way it's done in all the movies. I only hope this doesn't take too long. If we're not out of here by nine, we may see Madame Vandermeer's ugly face again. I hope she doesn't decide to set the whole house on fire this time."

Amy sensed great impending danger. She knew her ancestral cousin, Jebediah Tredwell, would never knowingly place her in jeopardy, but the idea of conjuring up another spirit made her uneasy. "I've never done this."

"This'll be the first time—and the *last*. I swear, Amy, if we ever get out of this one, you'd better—"

"Shhh, how can I concentrate if you keep talking?"

"Okay, do your stuff."

As Amy closed her eyes she felt a strange tingle run through her body. "I'm not sure what'll happen to me, Jamie," she said softly. "What if I pass out or something?"

"I'll take care of you; I promise. If things get out of control, I'll get you away from here. I swear—twins' honor."

Amy clasped her brother's hands tighter. "Okay, twins' honor." She took a few deep breaths, exhaling each one slowly, then concentrated on the darkness beyond her closed eyes. The odd tingling sensation became a strong vibration. Amy slowly opened her eyes and stared into the distance. She loosened her hold on Jamie's hands so that only their fingertips were touching. She sensed a concentrated stillness growing within her. "I wish to be the medium for the spirit of Henry Hudson to appear," she whispered. "We are two of us here. We wish to help the spirit of Turtledove pass on."

As Amy continued, a stillness descended on the room. "We are two of us here," she repeated. "We require the help of Henry Hudson."

The silence now seemed like a deafening buzz. Jamie stared at his sister. Her body had suddenly become rigid, and she sat bolt upright. Then her head fell backward, and her eyes began to roll up and down. "Hey, Amy, are you okay?" She did not reply. From the points at which their fingertips met, Jamie could feel the energy radiating from Amy's hands into his.

Then Amy's body began to shake uncontrollably as if a giant electric charge were racing through it. "What's happening?" Jamie asked with concern. "Are you all right? Listen, maybe we should forget this whole deal, okay?"

Amy began to open her mouth as if to reply. But the voice that emerged was not hers. The voice of a man came from within Amy's body: the deep, husky voice of a man. "Speak your names, you that call me forth," the Voice demanded. "Identify yourselves."

Jamie stared at his sister in amazement. He realized that technically Amy was no longer present and some other force had taken over.

"Speak your names," the voice repeated.

Jamie knew that he would have to speak for his sister and himself. "Our names are Amy and Jamie Ferguson."

"From whence do you come?"

"From whence? Oh, we come from the United States of America."

"The Americas? Yes, please to continue."

"Can I ask your name?"

"I have none as such. Names are not needed for those in astral form."

"Did you ever have a name? Did you ever live on earth?"

"I did."

"Is your—was your name Henry Hudson?"

Amy's head began to sway from side to side. "It was,"

said the Voice emerging from within her. "Tell me why you call me forth. Speak."

"Were you Hudson the explorer?"

"Yes, I was an explorer and navigator."

"Could you tell me something about your last voyage?"

Amy's head fell to her chest and she grew limp. When she raised her head again, her face had taken on a peculiar expression. "On the seventeenth of April, 1610, we broke ground and set sail from St. Katharine's Pool in the vessel the *Discovery*," the Voice began. "I had a crew of twenty-two, with Robert Juet as master's mate. Past the Orkneys, our course was due north. By July we'd arrived at the southern extremity of the bay from whence we viewed Labrador—a cold sterile grim country. From thence we sailed north once more for many months. In November our vessel was hauled aground, and we were frozen in. Our provisions were low and there was unrest among the crew."

"What was the reason for your journey?" Jamie asked.

"We hoped to find the Northwest Passage to the other ocean called the South Sea," the Voice explained. "But instead we sat in the frozen desolation of the great dead sea of the New World, where we subsisted upon birds caught by God's providence. But providence could not soften the hearts of my obdurate crew. The hour of my darkness was nigh."

"Do you mean the mutiny?"

The Voice grew louder: "They were an angry group of malcontents, hungry and undisciplined, who questioned my competence as a navigator. Wilson, the boatswain,

106

seized me from behind and pinioned my arms with a rope. In great haste the conspirators got the shallop to the ship's side and lowered me into it. Presently six of my crew were ordered to follow, as well as my son, John. Lastly, Philip Staffe, my carpenter, came down into our doomed boat with his chest of tools, his musket, some meal, and an iron pot."

"That's all you had for nine men in a little boat?"

"Yes, we were without food, drink, fire, clothing, or other necessities, set adrift by mariners with wrens' hearts. There we sat until we had become a speck on the cruel waves of the icy wilderness."

Amy's body went limp again, and the Voice ceased.

"No, don't go," Jamie said pleadingly. "I have a theory that you came ashore and met friendly Indians."

The Voice had become much weaker. "On previous voyages I had acquaintance with many friendly Indians in North America."

"That's what I thought," said Jamie. "Those carpenters' tools you had with you in the shallop would've been of interest to the Indians. With tools you could've landed somewhere and built shelter."

Though the Voice did not respond, Jamie was convinced his theory was correct. Hudson could have survived, met with friendly natives, and his son could have become a member of the tribe. That would explain the fair-skinned Indian who appeared in Hudson Bay so many years later. He might have been a direct descendant of Henry Hudson! And Turtledove was probably *his* direct descendant.

Amy's breathing changed its rhythm, and she began to pant, as if gasping for air. "This instrument is losing its energy," the Voice gasped. "I cannot tarry longer."

"No, wait," Jamie said urgently, "there's a spirit of an Indian girl present in this house. She has some connection with you and needs your help to pass on."

"What connection?" the Voice demanded.

"She may be a relative," Jamie explained.

"A descendant?"

"That's right, but she's trapped here on earth."

"A soul in torment? How may I aid her in her journey?"

"Maybe you already have," Jamie said. "Now we know Turtledove's secret, so I guess she can pass on. If Madame Vandermeer can't torment her any longer, *she'll* probably pass on too."

"Then 'tis done," the Voice said, almost inaudible as it had grown so weak. Amy gasped one final breath, then slumped down in the chair, totally limp. Jamie could see she was still in a trance, but he didn't know how to get her out of it.

"Wake up, Amy," he said, shaking her. "I think everything's okay now. Madame Vandermeer must be gone."

Suddenly a roaring gust of wind circled through the kitchen like a tornado. Then the ghost of Madame Vandermeer appeared in the doorway, her figure at the very eye of the turbulence she had produced. "You lie!" she shouted in rage, "this is my domain and those who inhabit it are subservient to me *forever!*"

The vengeful spirit raised her hands in the air, and all the copper pots and pans hanging from the beams hur-

108

tled across the room. Suddenly everything else in the room started to clatter and rumble. The ovens, freezers, blenders, and other kitchen equipment swirled around above the children's heads in a whirlwind of destruction. Even the terra-cotta tiles became uprooted from the floor and began bouncing off the walls.

"Mine!" cried Madame Vandermeer in exultation. "Mine to destroy if I so wish!"

Trying to protect himself, Jamie lunged underneath the table. As he did, the massive butcher block rose up into the air and hung there, suspended precariously above the children's heads.

Madame Vandermeer looked triumphant. "With a mere movement of my finger," she warned, "it shall smash you into pieces. Perhaps now you will acknowledge my power and begone from my domain forever."

Jamie felt paralyzed by indecision. He knew they would need all their joint concentration to negate Saskia's destructive powers, but Amy was still slumped in the chair, unconscious and unable to move. Her delicate trance state had left her at a point midway between two realities; she was totally defenseless. Jamie longed to escape, yet he refused to leave his sister behind.

Madame Vandermeer, enjoying her supreme control, toyed with her victims like a cat with two captive mice. She laughed maniacally as the huge butcher-block table teetered above the children's heads.

Jamie shook his sister, trying desperately to awaken her, but she would not regain consciousness.

"Enough!" Madame Vandermeer shouted. "I tire of

this charade. You amuse me no longer." And with that she lowered her hands, and the huge table began hurtling to the ground.

Jamie lunged toward the chair Amy was seated in, and tried to drag it to safety. But in the split second before the table fell, he could envision them being crushed beneath it. And then, strangely, time seemed to stop. In that moment beyond time *nothing* was inevitable; there were myriad potentials in the universe. The children could be saved from destruction, they *could*—if only—

Suddenly a white light radiated through the room, and the table ceased its furious hurtle and drifted weightlessly to the floor, dropping gently back into place. Jamie gasped as he saw the ghostly figure of an officer of the Continental Army standing beside the lady of the Manor. "Jebediah," he asked, "is it really you? I can't believe I can *see* you!"

Jebediah's form grew more visible. "Yes, 'tis I, James. And you must continue to believe, for it is that strength of belief which has summoned me hither."

Jamie was still confused. "I've never seen you before, but I knew you'd come to help us, I just *knew* it."

Jebediah drew closer to the boy. "It would seem we both have powers far beyond our knowledge."

"I sure hope so," Jamie said, and sighed; "because things are a real mess around here. We thought we had stuff under control, but—"

"Control?" shouted Madame Vandermeer. "Only *I* have control here. Who dares usurp my authority?" As she raised her hands above her head to evoke further havoc,

Jebediah extended his own, not in a gesture of defiance, but one of friendship.

"Come, Madame," he said politely, "this earthly place is no longer rightfully yours."

"You lie," Saskia shouted, "I am still the lady of the Manor, ever and for always." Suddenly the rage in Saskia's eyes subsided. She stared at the other spirit before her as if in recognition. "I believe I *know* you."

"Yes, Madame," Jeb replied. "I was once your guest in this house. Come," he repeated, offering Saskia his arm. "Cast off your jewels and earthly possessions so that you may enter into the realm of greater awareness as I have done."

Saskia rejected the spirit's gentlemanly offer. "No," she protested, "all these possessions are rightfully mine. No power can take them from me."

Jebediah was not to be undone. "Far greater possessions await you, Madame. Knowledge is the jewel of highest value. Come, won't you join me?"

A look of weariness replaced the anger in Saskia's eyes, as if the burden of protecting all she held dear had become too great.

"For more than two centuries you have stood guard over your earthly domain," Jebediah said sympathetically. "Cast off your burden now and follow me."

"Two centuries?" She sighed. "Has it truly been so long?"

"Indeed, Madame."

Saskia began to waver. "There will be riches in this place which awaits me?"

111

Jebediah smiled. "True riches, unlike those known on earth. You have merely to pass the portals and the journey shall begin."

Madame Vandermeer glanced around the room one final time, as if saying good-bye to all her earthly riches. "Yes, I do weary of this burden," she said. Finally acquiescing, she accepted Jebediah's arm. As he led her toward the door adjoining the garden, their figures began to dissolve into a filmy mist.

"Wait," Jamie shouted. "Is it all over now? Is Turtledove gone too?"

Jebediah's voice was barely audible. "She remains," he whispered. "Another must come for her, a far higher spirit than myself."

Amy moaned and turned over in the chair. She was beginning to regain consciousness. Now she opened her eyes. "What happened?" she whispered. "I feel so weak."

Jamie hardly knew where to begin. "It was fantastic. First you conjured up Henry Hudson, then Saskia wrecked the joint, but then *Jeb* appeared. I actually *saw* him, Amy, and he's just like you described him. Jeb came to take Madame Vandermeer away. You should've seen him; he was so polite, Saskia couldn't resist him. I guess we never thought of being *nice* to her, did we? Anyway, it worked and I bet she'll never come back here again."

Amy smiled weakly. "I knew you'd see Jeb someday, too, Jamie. I guess you had to *believe* first. But what happened to Turtledove?"

"That's still a mystery. Jeb said someone else would have to come for her—someone more powerful. Who could it be? I wonder. Anyway, I'm glad you're back because watching you in that trance was creepy. Your eyes rolled around like marbles and I thought you'd drop dead! Promise me that next time we hear a place is haunted we'll run like—" Jamie's words stuck in his throat as he watched his sister stare blankly into the distance. She had gone into another trance!

Amy slowly rose from the chair, placed herself cross-legged on the floor, and began pounding the floor with rhythmic drumbeats.

Jamie felt utterly helpless. "What's happening *now*?"

Amy could not hear him. She continued the steady drumming until it became louder and louder and the sound reverberated off the walls.

Jamie quickly glanced around, aware that the fire in the hearth had begun to blaze. There, huddled in the corner, he could see the spectral shape of the Indian girl, Turtledove. Her frostbitten body was shivering with cold. The girl whimpered in fear and pain as she reached her ghostly hand into flames that returned no warmth to her frozen apparition. After a moment Turtledove heard the rhythmic drumming and turned toward Amy.

Amy suddenly stopped pounding the floor and placed her hands on her knees. As she threw her head back, another strange voice began to emerge from within her body. "Oh, hear me," the Voice commanded. "I speak to you in the music of the wind, the singing of the grass, the whispering of the leaves, the rippling waters, the voices of the animals and the singing birds. Come, Oh Turtledove, I speak to you."

113

A faint smile formed across Turtledove's lips. She gripped her fists tightly to control her quivering body. "Kitchi Manitou, is it really you?"

"Yes, it is I, the Great Spirit. Like the sudden blinking of the bird's eye as he streaks through the sky, you shall know me. I make it possible for the spirits of the dead to cross over to the Shadow Land."

Now the girl's lips parted in terror and grief. "I cannot go," she cried. "The evil spirit of the fire holds me here."

"No one holds you any longer," replied the Great Spirit. "The eagle flies very high and can carry you upon its wings to the Great Place above."

Jamie stood in silence, afraid to interrupt. He kept staring at Turtledove, but she wouldn't move. Something still held her trapped in her netherworld. "Is it time?" she asked.

"It is time," replied the Great Spirit. "You have been dead for many suns, little chief. The four seasons have often come and gone. Many sleeps and snows have passed. Many moons have faded since your journey from the Land of Many Waters." Amy's head dropped down like the broken wing of a bird. When she looked up again, the spirit voice within her spoke with compassion and great understanding. "Come, little sister, let your heart fly to the Great Spirit."

Turtledove remained motionless, still trapped beside the fire.

"What holds you here, little chief?" asked the Great Spirit.

"There is no one to mourn my going," she explained.

"Those who are here shall mourn you and remember, for the Great Spirit is in all things. Come. The wind shall blow and the thunderbird shall flap its wings, for I have spoken."

Turtledove slowly rose from her place beside the fire. A look of peace and acceptance crossed her face as she spoke. "I have heard your words, Kitchi Manitou; I shall come. I hear the song within my heart and I shall follow."

As Turtledove reached out her hands, the flames within the hearth rose up and transformed her into a glowing white-winged bird. The apparition fluttered across the room, then hovered above Amy's head for a moment. Then it was gone.

Jamie stared, dumbfounded, as ashes spewed from the hearth and formed themselves into a pattern on the floor. He slowly walked over to read the one-word message: "PEACE."

Chapter Sixteen

ONLY A FEW MINUTES HAD PASSED SINCE THE FINAL SPIRIT HAD vacated Vandermeer Manor, but to Jamie it seemed like an eternity. As Amy sat motionless on the floor, he anxiously awaited her return from the trance state.

Finally Amy put her hands to her eyes and rubbed them as if she had awakened from a deep sleep. "Jamie," she whispered drowsily, "are you here?"

"Right here," he said. "How are you?"

"I'm okay, I guess, but I feel so strange—as if I'd been on a long journey to places I can't remember." Amy felt physically weary, but she sensed in herself a new inner awareness and well-being.

"Well, it's all over now." Jamie sighed with relief. "Now that both ghosts are gone, things are back to normal."

116

"No, it's not over yet," she replied, "we haven't finished."

Jamie gulped. "Don't go into another trance, *please*. I can't take any more; this séance stuff is making me a nervous wreck!"

"Don't worry," said Amy, "the trance is over. But there's something we have to finish and you have to help me." Amy walked to the hearth and swept the ashes into a dustpan, then placed them in a small glass jar. "C'mon, we have to bury these. Let's do it quickly before Uncle Harold gets back."

The twins opened the kitchen door and strolled out into the cool, moist night air. With a spoon Amy overturned the damp loose ground beside the lilac bush, then buried the jar. "Farewell, Turtledove," she began to chant. She covered the spot with earth. "You are now on the bank of the Great River from which you can hear the singing of another country. In this country all is delightful and it is never cold." She turned toward Jamie. "Say it with me," she insisted.

Jamie knelt beside his sister and repeated the chant. "Farewell, Turtledove. You are now on the bank of the Great River from which you can hear—" Jamie stopped. Their uncle had walked up behind them! Uncle Harold and his accountant, Mr. Dudley, were staring down at the twins with interest. Through the semidarkness Jamie could see the quizzical expression on their faces.

"What's this?" Harold asked. "An evening ceremony left over from your youthful days at camp?"

"Ceremony?" Jamie asked innocently. "Us? What a

funny thing to say, Uncle Harry." He stood up and brushed the moist soil from his jeans.

"What'd you kids bury there?" Mr. Dudley asked.

"Nothing," said Jamie.

"A mouse," said Amy.

"Nothing but a mouse," Jamie added. "We found it lying dead in the kitchen. We didn't want Bridget to freak out when she returns, so we got rid of it."

"That's right," Amy said. "Poor Bridget has been frightened enough, but now things are back to normal."

"I certainly hope not!" Harold said excitedly. "I've just told Fred all about the visions you kids have been seeing around here. He wanted to come by and meet you both. Aside from being my accountant, Fred has a production company and he's very interested in what you had to say."

"That's right," explained Fred Dudley. "Harold was worried about going broke with this place, but I told him not to worry. If he's got real ghosts up here, he can make a fortune! Have you kids really seen horrible visions?"

"Visions?" Amy repeated. "Us?"

"Yes, *you*," Harold snapped. "The rotting flesh, the Indian girl, the icebergs, the fires. You told me all about it earlier."

Fred Dudley was thrilled. "It all sounds terrific. People with genuine haunted houses can make a bundle. I'll get someone to ghostwrite—pardon the expression—a book about your experiences. Then we'll turn it into a screenplay and make a million. Have you got any black ooze coming out of your water pipes? That's always good. A

118

guy in Long Island made a *fortune* from his haunted property. Horror is big business, you know. That guy had tons of black stuff oozing out of *everything*."

"There's no ooze around here," Amy said. "In fact, everything's fine."

"Perfectly fine," Jamie said. "I guess Uncle Harry has a lively imagination."

"And the heebie-jeebies," Amy added.

"I *what*?" Harold was indignant. "Didn't you kids tell me— Look, I was cooking pancakes, and you guys came in and—" Harold scratched his head. "Oh, never mind."

"You mean there are no ghosts?" Fred Dudley asked disappointedly. "Not even one?"

"Not even one," Amy said, certain that statement was true at last.

Mr. Dudley shrugged. "Too bad, Harry, we could've made a mint. Well, look on the bright side. Without any bona fide ghosts, you're back in business again."

Chapter Seventeen

OVERNIGHT THE CLOUD OF SUSPICION AND APPREHENSION THAT had hovered over Vandermeer Manor had suddenly lifted.

Bridget returned the next morning to take up her station in the kitchen. After a careful inspection of every nook and cranny of her domain, she pronounced it free from all unearthly presences. "Clean as a whistle, Master Harold. Whatever was here has come and gone."

The twins hoped Harold would be pleased by the news. But their uncle still clung to the faint hope of making a million-dollar movie deal. "Did you check the microwave?" he asked hopefully. "Any snowballs?"

"I told you, sir; everything's fine. Maybe some mischievous spirit played a few pranks, then left. They do that sometimes, goodness knows. But from now on, nothing goes into that oven but my home cooking!"

"What's wrong, Uncle Harold?" Amy asked. "You looked disappointed."

"Me? Of course not. I just can't figure out what went on here—or when it stopped—or *why*."

"It was probably a hallucination," Jamie offered.

"Or mass hysteria," Amy added. "Things like that happen sometimes, don't they?"

Harold stared at the twins. He could not shake the feeling that they both knew more than they would ever admit. "Sure," he said, "*anything* can happen, I guess. But what could've made you kids think you saw such horrible visions?"

Neither Amy nor Jamie could think of a reasonable reply. "Well, twins act crazy sometimes," Amy said. "That's a documented fact. At least once a year all twins see something crazy."

"They do?" Harold asked.

"Sure," Jamie said, "it's in all the psychology books. Maybe it has something to do with our brains being so close together. It's called twins syndrome."

"Is that a fact," Bridget said with interest. "I never heard such a thing."

"Neither have I," said Harold, smiling. He winked at the twins. "Okay, we'll drop the subject. From now on, as far as I'm concerned, there's no such thing as a ghost— real, imagined or *hired*."

"Hired?" said Bridget. "What a funny thing to say, sir. How can you hire a ghost?"

There was a twinkle in Harold's eye. "Never mind, old girl. We all have our little secrets, but now they're ancient history. Let's get this show on the road, okay? I'm expecting three new guests to arrive at noon. Today three guests, tomorrow the world! I'll be back in the chips again in no time."

By evening the entire staff had returned. It seemed as if they had all received some miraculous message that the Manor was now a safe and pleasant place. And so it was. By eight o'clock the Dining Hall was filled. Many of the dinner guests were making plans to spend the night.

Harold knew better than to question whatever supernatural forces may or may not have been instrumental in his good fortune. He returned to his duties as host, mingling with his guests and making polite conversation.

At nine o'clock when the chimes of the grandfather clock rang out through the Manor, dinner was in progress and all that could be heard over the clock's chimes were the clinking of glasses and the carefree conversation of the happy crowd.

Jamie, seated at a corner table, breathed a deep sigh of relief. At last his vacation could begin. He had several more days to live like a king, in the lap of luxury. Maybe Uncle Harry would drive him into town in the Porsche and stop at the shopping mall. Jamie had seen a terrific pair of jogging shoes, which would come in handy. And some new tennis balls. And shorts, too, not to mention—

Embarrassed by his greedy thoughts, Jamie glanced across the room toward the portrait of Saskia Vandermeer. Her image had lost its imperious quality. Perhaps it was his imagination, but Jamie thought the portrait's features had softened. Yes, he saw the faint beginnings of a knowing smile encircling Saskia's lips—a smile that had not been there before.

After dinner Amy took a walk around the grounds of the Manor. The mountains surrounding the property were almost palpable presences in the inviting darkness. Amy stood quietly listening to the night sounds. Trees rustled, insects chattered, and the rippling waters of the lake lapped against the shore. And there were sounds behind the sounds, audible if one listened intently, as Amy did now. Was that a barely perceptible drumbeat echoing across the valley? A ghostly echo long gone from the mountains, it seemed to linger just beyond earshot, somewhere very far away.

Amy smiled to herself and continued her walk. As she passed the kitchen she heard Bridget humming softly as she removed her chokecherry pies from the oven. Their aroma hung in the air, mingling with the tantalizing outdoor scents.

Amy walked toward the lilac bush where she and Jamie had buried the jar of ashes. She knelt down, stroking her hands over the moist, newly overturned earth. There in the damp ground Amy felt something soft and warm. She picked it up and examined it by the light of the kitchen window. It was the single white feather of a turtledove.

As she stroked it a plaintive bird's song could be heard faintly in the distance. As she listened to the far-off melody, Amy remembered the words from The Song of

Solomon: "For, lo, the winter is past, . . . and the voice of the turtle is heard in our land."

Feeling a strange combination of sadness and joy, Amy slipped the feather into her pocket. She waved to Bridget, then slowly walked back toward the Manor.